ARCHITECTS OF DESTINY

By Amy DuBoff

ARCHITECTS OF DESTINY
Copyright © 2015 Amy DuBoff

Published by BDL Press
Editor: Nicholas Bubb
Cover Illustration: Copyright © 2015 Tom Edwards

ISBN: 0692589120
ISBN-13: 978-0692589120
Copyright Registration Number: TXu001958485

0 9 8 7 6 5 4 3 2

Produced in the United States of America

To my Bay

CONTENTS

PART 1: NEW BEGINNINGS

◄ CHAPTER 1 ►

I must leave tonight. I can't stay here any longer— Cris Sietinen ducked to avoid the electronic rapier swinging toward his head.

"Stay focused." His tutor jumped to the side as he stabbed at Cris' torso.

Cris parried the blow, a challenging glint in his cobalt eyes. "You haven't hit me yet."

"You haven't struck me, either." His tutor circled him, steel-blue eyes locked on Cris. "Get inside your opponent's head, just as Marina taught you. Movements can deceive, but what's in the mind can't be faked. Trust your intuition."

Clearing his thoughts, Cris prepared for a telepathic assessment. "It's not intuition, Sedric. Science has told us that much."

Sedric Almar sighed. "Telepathy, clairvoyance, call it what you will. You are one of the few with the gift. Use it." He took a swing toward Cris' right leg. Though decades past his prime, he still possessed the same youthful vigor as the day he joined the Tararian Guard. Now a trusted Captain, he remained a formidable opponent in any close-quarter combat, gray hair or not.

With his mind cleared, Cris reached out to read the thoughts grazing the surface of Sedric's consciousness—catching a glimpse of his next move. Before his instructor could complete his swing, Cris deflected the attack. "If it's such a 'gift', then why does everyone treat it like a curse?"

"Don't be so dramatic." Sedric jabbed toward the main sensor on the chest of Cris' training jumpsuit.

As he dodged the attack, Cris brought his own blade to Sedric's collar in one fluid motion. The sensor lights illuminated red. A kill hit.

Sedric held out his hands in defeat and nodded his approval. "Next time I won't go easy on you."

Cris took a step back to rest. "I can't solely rely on telepathy to win. There must be a reason the Priesthood condemns the use of such abilities." His covert lessons from Marina were defiant enough, flirting with the boundaries of legality.

Sedric reset his jumpsuit using the controls on the sleeve, and the sensors returned to blue. "It's not our place to speculate about matters regarding the Priesthood. Not even yours, my lord."

"But you have to wonder," Cris pondered. "On Tararia and most of the colonies, there's nothing but anti-telekinesis propaganda. Yet, an entire division of the TSS is dedicated to honing the abilities of those rare 'gifted' individuals, and the Priesthood does nothing."

"The Tararian Selective Service is unique in many ways," Sedric replied, dismissing the dispute with a shake of his head. He gripped his sword and took an offensive stance. "Now, we have a lesson to finish."

Cris was resolute, determined to finally get an answer to the questions his teacher was always so eager to dodge. *This is my last chance before I leave.* "You spent a year with the TSS, didn't you? You must have seen so much—"

A single crease deepened between Sedric's dark eyebrows. "My lord, with all respect, your father doesn't appreciate discussion of the TSS."

Cris' restraint slipped. "Of course he doesn't. He wants me to ignore my abilities, just like he did. Why should I listen to someone who wants me to live a lie?"

"I'm sorry, I—" Sedric brought his slender sword to a resting position with the illuminated tip on the ground.

Cris fought to maintain composure, but his serene façade shattered. "You don't understand what it's like… to have all the privileges of being born into this family, and yet it doesn't mean anything. He'll never be happy with who I am, not after the son he lost years ago. Me? I'm just his replacement heir to the Sietinen Dynasty—a tool to perpetuate our familial empire." *A disappointing shadow of the brother I never knew.*

"You mustn't think that way, my lord," Sedric said with a gentleness that belied his hardened exterior.

Stars! Just a few more hours… Cris swallowed, his throat tight. *Then I can get away from Tararia and stop being compared to the impossibly perfect memory of Tristen.* "Shite, it's no wonder he and Mother avoid me. I guess by now I should be used to seeing my instructors more than my own parents." Cris met Sedric's gaze for a moment before looking down.

Sedric put an encouraging hand on Cris' toned shoulder. "You're true to yourself, and that's the best thing you can be."

Like that's done me any good so far. Cris undid the collar of his dark gray training jumpsuit, extinguishing the subtle blue sensor lights. "I've had enough for today."

Sedric nodded, but his jaw was set in a frown.

Cris stepped from the black rubberized tiles covering the training arena onto the veined, white marble found throughout the estate. He set his sword in its rack along the wall next to the other training weapons. As he removed his jumpsuit, he stared out the window at the clear sky above the manicured grounds. He couldn't wait to be out among the stars.

To Cris' disappointment, when he glanced at the time displayed on the viewscreen integrated into the wall, he saw that it was only halfway through the scheduled lesson time. He sighed.

Sedric rested both hands atop the hilt of his sword. "Why the sudden interest in the TSS?"

Cris returned to the arena, wearing only the gray t-shirt and black workout pants that had been beneath his training attire. "It's a significant institution, but all I ever hear are rumors. You were actually there. What was it really like?"

"Very different than anything here on Tararia," his instructor replied after a moment.

"How so?"

Sedric scowled. "You're trying to get me in trouble."

"This is just between us, I promise."

The Captain eyed him, still on edge. "First off, nothing of anyone's life outside the TSS mattered. You could come from one of the High Dynasties or from the streets—everyone was treated the same." He paused, but Cris' pleading eyes drove him on. He smoothed his light gray uniform as if reliving a morning muster. "Though I was just in the Militia division, I had a few chances to meet the Agents. They have this presence that can quiet a room. Such power. I was always awed by their abilities. It was something timeless."

Cris was captivated. *Unrestricted telekinesis… What can they do?* "So why did you leave?"

A grimace flitted across Sedric's face, barely perceptible. "Many only attend for the first year. It just wasn't the life for me."

Cris examined his instructor. "If many leave after the first year, it must be easy to join. How do—"

Sedric let out a gruff laugh. "Oh, I see! I never should have said anything. Now you're getting fanciful ideas."

A disarming smile brought out Cris' natural good looks. He ran a hand through his chestnut brown hair. "Please, Sedric? I'm only trying to broaden my knowledge of the outside world."

His teacher scrutinized him. "There's an open application process for Militia, but most Agent slots are by invitation.

However, it is best if you permanently remove such thoughts from your mind."

Cris composed his face, but the mischievous smile never fully left his eyes. "I was just curious."

The old guard was not convinced. "You have a duty, my lord. Whether you like it or not, you are the Sietinen heir and will one day be in charge of SiNavTech and the Third Region of Tararia. That is an extraordinary responsibility. I only hope that you will embrace that power."

"Oh, I will, eventually." *Just as I will embrace the power that I have within.* "But I'm only sixteen—that's still a long ways off."

Sedric was about to respond, but was interrupted by the door opening.

Cris turned to see who had entered. His gaze rested on Marina Alexri, one of his father's Court Advisors; the intrusion did nothing to improve his mood. Marina was in her mid-twenties and pretty, but she had a frigid demeanor that could silence a room. Her station as his sole telepathy instructor was the one redeeming element of their relationship. He instinctively bolstered his ever-present mental guards, careful to bury his plans for that night. *Stars! What does she want?*

"Working hard with combat techniques, I see," Marina said, gliding forward. Her dark blonde hair was pulled up into a complex bun with braids and twists, and she wore a rich emerald dress tailored to her slender figure. Her green eyes surveyed the room, missing no detail.

Sedric came to attention. "We were exploring the finer points of verbal battle, madam."

"Naturally." Marina smiled curtly. "Come, Cristoph. There is a matter your father must discuss with you."

"It's 'Cris'," he corrected, despite failing with his hundreds of previous attempts.

"As you wish, my lord." The Court Advisor withdrew from the room.

When Marina was out of sight, Cris let out a slow breath and turned to Sedric. "I'm sorry for arguing. You're a wonderful teacher. I don't mean to be difficult." His throat constricted. *You're the only one I'll miss… You always believed in me.*

Sedric beamed. "Think nothing of it, my lord."

Marina returned to the doorway. "Come along. Your father is waiting." She disappeared again.

Cris smiled one last time at Sedric before he followed Marina, trying to ease the knot in his chest.

"I'm surprised my father sent you to fetch me. Now you're running errands for him?" Cris asked the Court Advisor as he approached. Since coming into the employ of the Sietinen Dynasty three years before, Marina was almost always posted in one of the administrative offices throughout the estate to oversee dynastic operations. Cris' twice-weekly telepathy lessons over the last year were one of the few exceptions.

Marina's brow twitched. "Actually, in light of a recent development, he wished me to terminate your telepathy instruction. I thought that best said in person."

Those lessons had been the one thing Cris was reluctant to give up when he thought about leaving his home. If that was being taken away, there was truly nothing left for him on Tararia. "I see."

"Such training was an unnecessary distraction," Marina continued. "It's time to focus on what matters."

Except, what mattered to Cris was of no concern to the rest of his family. *All the more reason to leave now while I still can.* He shook his head and looked down.

The Court Advisor pursed her lips. "What are you hiding?"

Cris quickly suppressed the thoughts of his upcoming departure. "Do you really want to know?"

Marina rolled her eyes and set off down the corridor. "Come along. We're late."

Cris stood his ground. "On second thought, I'm not in the

mood for another lecture. I think I'll pass on the father-son chat."

Marina spun around on her heel to glare at Cris. "How can you be so flippant? You know he's busy. Someone has to tend to all of the political and economic issues *you've* never bothered to understand—"

Cris crossed his arms. *Oh, don't I? Try quizzing me sometime and we'll see who knows what.*

"—and to oversee this Region, all while leading the transportation industry for known civilization… You should be more appreciative of the time you get with him." She flourished her arms with exasperation. "Honestly, Cristoph, you become more insolent every time I see you."

That's because I can't take feeling like an outcast in my own family anymore. "Sorry. I guess I just have insurmountable faults in my personality."

Marina's eyes narrowed.

Cris glared back. "Since I'll apparently be berated anywhere I go, you may as well lead me straight to my father so I can get the worst of it out of the way."

The Court Advisor let out a huff and resumed striding down the hallway.

No snide response? I'll count that as a win. Cris followed her at a safe distance.

As he trailed Marina through the spacious corridors of the Sietinen mansion's southern wing, he glimpsed the landscaped grounds of the estate through towering windows overlooking the city of Sieten below and the great Lake Tiadon in the distance. Sieten, the capital city of the Third Region, was nestled in the breathtaking foothills of the Bethral Mountains. Its temperate climate was pleasant in the peaks of summer and winter even without weather modification, making it envied by Dynasties throughout the five other Regions of Tararia. Though it was the only home Cris had ever known, he still felt the need to get away and see what the galaxy had to offer. *I'll come back eventually. I just want to find myself while I still have the chance.*

Marina and Cris arrived at the palatial outer administrative office for the Head of the Sietinen Dynasty. The attendants and advisors throughout the room looked to be working furiously at various touch-surface computer consoles and desktop holodisplays, though Cris had doubts about how much was actually being accomplished.

Cris spotted his father. He, like all Sietinens before, had the distinctive chestnut hair and striking cobalt eyes that defined the bloodline; carefully arranged marriages ensured the continuation of these traits. Cris knew his mother's Talsari heritage was nearly as pure as Sietinen, but the prestige of Sietinen was paramount.

Marina led Cris toward the elder Sietinen, who was absorbed in conversation with two advisors. To Cris' displeasure, Marina halted just beyond earshot of his father's conversation, leaving Cris to stand idly while the exchange concluded. How typical, after all the rush to arrive for the meeting, Cris would still have to wait. He glanced over at Marina. She returned his gaze with a decidedly hostile smile.

After a few minutes, the advisors were dismissed and Reinen Sietinen-Monsari turned to look Cris over silently. Gray touched his temples, bringing a sense of distinguished age to his handsome features. He wore a deep blue suit embellished with silver accents, the finest available. "Marina informed you of the change to your instruction, I presume."

"Hello to you, too, father," Cris replied. "Yes, she told me."

Reinen nodded. "Let's go into my office."

Cris followed his father into a smaller room off to the right. Reinen sat down on a sleek brown couch near the center of the room and gestured for Cris to sit in one of the upholstered chairs across from him. Behind them, a desk was framed by an arched window that stretched nearly the width of the room, looking directly over Lake Tiadon. The sun was beginning its descent, shadows emphasizing the features of the lush landscape.

"Why the sudden end to my lessons with Marina?" Cris asked as he sat down.

Reinen's eyes narrowed the slightest measure. "You've already learned enough to guard yourself. There's nothing further to explore."

"Would a little object levitation really hurt anyone?"

His father leaned forward, stern. "The laws apply to you, too. We're supposed to be setting an example as leaders."

"Right, by supporting the policies that make it illegal to learn about oneself."

Reinen grunted. "Maybe you should take the matter up with the Priesthood."

Cris was about to brush off the statement, but there was a seriousness in his father's tone. "What do you mean?"

"I received a communiqué this afternoon. The Priesthood has requested a meeting with you."

Cris froze. "Why?" *Stars! Did they find out about my telepathy lessons?* His pulse spiked. Marina's instruction had always stayed within the governing restrictions around telepathy, but if they suspected Cris had crossed the line into telekinesis, there was no telling what the meeting might entail. He gulped.

"The representative only stated that they want to interview you as soon as possible." Reinen shook his head. "Whatever it's regarding, it's not the kind of attention we need."

Cris was well aware how rare it was to be singled out as an individual. The Priesthood of the Cadicle oversaw all Taran affairs, governing even the High Dynasties and their respective corporations that were the pillars for inter-planetary society. The organization served as the critical moderator to regulate the Taran worlds, controlling laws, the flow of information, and the application of new technological advances. Even lending the tiebreaking vote on any matter brought before the six High Dynasties, the Priesthood's authority was complete and binding. But, given its roots as a formerly theological institution, the Priesthood had been unquestionably viewed as Taran society's moral compass for generations.

"Did you set an appointment?" Cris asked, holding his breath that it wouldn't impact his departure plans.

"No. They wanted the interview to take place on their island, but I refused. The representative said he'd get back to me with alternate arrangements."

Cris let out his breath. *No matter now. I'll be gone by morning.* Cris felt his father's eyes on him and looked up.

"You're getting older, Cris. People are beginning to take more of an interest in you."

"You mean dynastic heads are trying to marry me off to their daughters. I'm still way too young to have any interest in such matters."

His father sighed. "One day soon you will have to."

"But not yet."

"Cris, I— I just worry about you."

Why does he pretend? At least Mother just ignores me. "Is that so? Forgive my incredulous tone, but it's just that you've never expressed much interest in me before."

Reinen seemed taken aback, his brow furrowed. "What makes you say that?"

Cris shook his head. "It doesn't matter."

"No, Cris, if something is bothering you, I want to know about it."

Cris sighed. "Now, when you say you worry about me... What do you mean—my political future? My future as the leader of this dynasty and as an executive of SiNavTech?"

"Well, of course. You seem disinterested."

That's because I am! "What about my feelings as your son?"

"I always assumed you were content."

"Content"… What about feeling loved? "Well, I'm not. I can't say I ever really was."

Reinen was silent for a long time. "I'm sorry."

Cris shrugged. *No he's not. He wouldn't have done anything differently.* "No matter now."

Reinen's expression was impassive.

"I know I'm not the one you wanted to be your successor." Cris' words hung in the air.

Reinen said nothing, but looked down, his face contorted in an attempt to hide his anguish.

"If there's nothing more, I'll return to my studies."

There was the slightest shake of Reinen's head. "No. There's nothing else."

That was your last chance to salvage any of your parental dignity. Without another word, Cris left his father's office and went directly to his living quarters.

Cris passed through the lounge area of his suite and stepped onto the generous balcony. A calm breeze ruffled his hair, cooled by the lake below. He breathed in the pure air. For a moment, he felt a twinge of regret. But, he knew staying on Tararia wouldn't do anyone good.

The idea of running away from his dynastic life first came to Cris more than two years before. He had been secretly preparing for the past six months, and almost everything was staged. All that remained was getting off the planet.

Cris returned to his bedroom and activated the touch-surface workstation on his desk. Settling into his chair, he began what had become a routine exercise of hacking into the secure central system for the Sietinen estate. Though not particularly easy, part of Cris' grooming had involved study of the complex system, so he knew shortcuts through the security blocks.

Once inside the system, he created an alias under the guise of a high-ranking guard and catalogued it in the central computer. Using the alias, he checked out a transport vessel at a secluded port on the southern side of the Sietinen compound. It would be waiting for him at midnight on the twenty-five hour Tararian clock. He also set up a standard maintenance reboot of the central security system to correspond with his departure. If he timed it right, he could slip out undetected and be well on his way before anyone knew he was gone.

With the final pieces of his departure plan in place, Cris admired one final sunset out his bedroom window. By daybreak, he'd be in space.

◄   CHAPTER 2   ►

It was 24:45. The world outside Cris' window was dark. Only the glow from Tararia's two moons, Aeris and Denae, illuminated the sky.

Dressed in plain street clothes, Cris gathered his provisions. Only a select few knew the electronic frequencies needed to illuminate the normally invisible identifying Dynastic Mark on his arm or read his imbedded ID chip, so all he needed to do was blend in. If he looked the part, he could become anyone he wanted.

Cris was accustomed to slipping out to walk the gardens in the middle of the night, but never had the stakes been so high. *They'll put me on complete lockdown if I'm caught leaving. No second chance.*

He crept from his quarters into the corridor. As a precaution, he reset the door's electronic lock so there would be no record of what time he left. He peered into the dimmed hallway. Clear. He ventured toward the nearest exit. The security system reboot was still five minutes away, set for 24:50 and scheduled to take twenty minutes. To avoid triggering alarms in the meantime, he used the less monitored servant passageways. He encountered no one, to his relief, and was soon outside.

Cris broke into a light jog along the main path that ran the length of the mansion. He made it no more than ten meters when he caught sight of a surveillance light. *Hide!*

He dove off the path into some bushes. The branches scraped at his bare face and hands, but he found a hollow within the foliage. He quickly retrieved a scrambler from the front pocket of his travel bag and activated the device; it should be enough to throw off the guard's sensors. He checked the time on his watch: 24:52. It was within the reboot window for the central system. He would be fine as long as he stayed out of sight.

Cris nearly held his breath as the guard approached. He could make out the armored form through the leaves, made more imposing under the moonlight. The guard was walking slowly, inspecting a handheld. He stopped in front of Cris.

Stars! Cris' heart raced. He stayed motionless, barely breathing.

The guard tapped the screen on his handheld a few times, then muttered something under his breath. After another minute, he continued strolling down the path in the direction Cris had come from.

Cris breathed a sigh of relief. When the guard was well past, he carefully extracted himself from the bushes and looked around to make sure no other guards were nearby. No one else was in sight. He smoothed his hair and brushed off a couple of leaves that had affixed to his jacket.

Cris returned to the path and resumed jogging toward the ship port. Excitement welled up in his chest, but he kept it at bay. *I'm not free yet.*

He reached the port at 24:57. Half a dozen shuttles occupied a paved area amid the foliage of the grounds. Each craft was approximately six meters long, with streamlined aerodynamics specifically designed for breaking through the planet's atmosphere.

Cris was about to enter the port when he spotted a figure in the small shelter used by port attendants during the day. He froze. There wasn't supposed to be anyone there overnight. His entire plan rested on using an automated kiosk to check out the shuttle under his guard alias. Needing to interact with a person changed everything.

He bit his lower lip, thinking. *I can't turn back now.* Seeing no other option, he strode confidently into the port and headed straight for the kiosk. He kept his face oriented away from the shelter.

The kiosk was dangerously close to the building, and it didn't take long for the attendant to rouse.

"What may I do for you?" the attendant asked.

Cris kept his head turned to the side so the attendant couldn't see his face. *I have every reason to be here. I'm in control.* "Official business," he said, faking a deeper voice. "You can verify my credentials on your own screen."

The attendant crossed his arms. "I'd like to see some ID."

Don't panic. Cris continued walking toward the kiosk with feigned assurance. "And I'd like to report you to your supervisor for impeding an official investigation. I don't think you want that on your performance record so close to review time."

"Your ID, sir," the attendant requested again.

Cris reached the kiosk. "I'll get it, hold it." Before the attendant could protest, Cris brought up his shuttle reservation in a few quick taps. He entered the access key for his guard alias. "There, satisfied?"

The attendant glanced at the authorization on the screen inside the shelter. "It checks out." He seemed unsure.

"So, do I need to have that chat with your supervisor?" Cris turned toward his assigned shuttle.

"No, sir," the attendant said. "Have a good night."

Cris let out a slow breath as he set off toward his shuttle. *We really need better security.*

The assigned shuttle was at the end of the row. Cris went to the far side of his craft and entered his specified passcode to open the main door. Once inside, he stowed his pack in a cargo area behind the eight passenger seats in the main cabin.

Cris moved to the cockpit to initiate the startup sequence. The touchscreen controls and holographic interfaces cast a cool glow in the cockpit. As the system ran its automated check, Cris strapped into the pilot's chair. He suppressed another wave of excitement.

When the shuttle was ready, Cris deftly lifted the vessel off the ground and launched it into space. Flight lessons had always been his favorite. He savored the exhilaration as the engine surged, feeling the power through the low vibrations in the controls. The muted rumble intensified as he pointed the vessel upward, locking in his destination. As he gained elevation, he became just one of many ships scattered throughout the night sky.

The acceleration of the vessel slowed as the sky turned from deep blue to black. Cris felt the artificial gravity automatically activate when the shuttle achieved orbit, settling his stomach.

I'm actually leaving Tararia. He relaxed just enough to smile. *But I still have a long way to go.*

Cris passed through one of the gates in the planetary shield and followed the course to the primary space station orbiting the planet. He sent a preset message requesting docking clearance. An affirmative response came immediately, and control of the shuttle was handed over to remote operators at the station.

Once the remote pilot took over, Cris allowed himself time to admire Tararia from above. *It's so beautiful from space—so peaceful.* Sieten was a mere speck of light on the western edge of the massive Third Region in the northern hemisphere, with the smaller Fourth, Fifth and Sixth Regions below it to the south. Across the sea to the west, he could see the edge of the crescent-shaped Second Region and the First Region to its south. In the sea between the Third and First regions was an island Cris knew to be the seat of the Priesthood. From space it seemed very small for someplace so important.

His shuttle was drawn into docking position and clamps locked onto the hull. Apprehension replaced his excitement as the small vessel shuddered under the docking clamps. It was the first time Cris had ever been off-world on his own, and preparing for such an adventure was never part of his lessons. He set his jaw, determined to not let nerves get the better of him. *I need to find a ship.*

Cris gathered his pack and made his way down the gangway into the space station. He was struck by the metallic quality of the filtered air, a harsh contrast to the fresh breeze off the lake. The foreign feeling of the station was heightened by an intense energy permeating the structure, felt both in the air and through the metal deck plates underfoot. The sub-audible hum of motors and electricity felt oppressive at first, but he centered himself and soon let the vibrations wash over him. He moved from the gangway into the main corridor of the concourse, where smooth metal walls arched overhead toward the center of a massive ring. Gangways stretched out to ships along the perimeter, and several broad concourses branched out to other rings with even more ships. Cris admired the sweeping metal forms through windows overhead and along the sides of the passageway. Even more wondrous was the blackness of space beyond, with dazzling stars holding untold possibilities.

The space station was more populated than Cris had anticipated for the late hour, but he had to remind himself that space travel didn't follow the same schedule as his home time zone. People moved about their business in the corridor, paying no attention to Cris as he eased into the flow of the foot traffic. Everyone was moving quickly, and where there were no openings in the crowd, someone would shove their way through. Cris found himself jostled as he tried to navigate the steady stream of travelers.

Just as he was starting to get comfortable, he was pushed

from behind. His bag came loose from his shoulder and almost fell to the floor. He took a few rapid steps to regain his balance, eventually catching himself on the wall of the corridor. He looked around.

A large man with cropped, thinning hair and a dingy jacket was cutting his way through the mass. Others stepped to the side to make way without missing a step. It was orchestrated chaos, and everyone but Cris knew the rhythm.

Cris pressed his back against the wall, trying to get his bearings again. A couple of people glanced over at Cris, but he may as well have been a decorative plant based on their reactions. He took a deep breath. *Don't fight the crowd.*

With an assertive stride, Cris reentered the stream of travelers. He had two more near-collisions but managed to avoid any further incidents. Following overhead signs, he made his way to the nearest directory where he could access the status of all ships at the port.

The directory was located in a bay off the central corridor. It was surrounded by an even denser throng of travelers. Cris spotted what looked to be a queue and took his place in the group. After several minutes, he noticed that people kept cutting in to take an open station when one became available. His face flushed with frustration. *They have no sense of order.*

Another person pushed ahead to grab a terminal at the directory, knocking Cris to the side. Cris tightened his grip on the bag over his shoulder. *I guess I need to act like them.*

A moment later, when a woman tried to push past Cris, he firmly held his place. The woman relaxed and waited behind him.

Cris took the next available terminal. He pulled up the transport directory, first looking over the outbound passenger transports. There were over a dozen cruisers to choose from, ranging from economical to luxurious. However, those would certainly be the first place anyone would look for him. Cris closed out of the list. That left the cargo freighters, and he found there were at least six times as many of those. Far too many choices. He filtered out all of the ships with large-volume, hazardous, or unregistered cargo. After discounting any with scheduled departures in more than one hour, only two potentials remained. *I should check them out in person before making a final selection.* He made a mental note of the docking coordinates for the two ships and cleared his search on the terminal, moving aside as someone lunged forward to use it.

Cris returned to the central corridor and made his way toward the docking location of the first ship. As he approached, he immediately felt uneasy, an instinct which Sedric and Marina always encouraged him to heed. Some members of the ship's crew were standing near the entrance to the gangway. They watched him pass, a touch of malice in their gaze. He moved on.

The second ship looked far more promising. Only a single man was near the entrance gangway, working on a tablet. He looked to be about sixty-years-old, and was somewhat grizzled. Attached to his belt was a red and white badge with his credentials, marking him as the ship's captain. Cris stood back and watched as another man exited the ship and engaged in conversation. *What are they talking about?*

Carefully, Cris reached out telepathically toward the two men. Though his abilities were not yet well developed, he was able to gather a few impressions. The captain seemed good natured, and he was on friendly terms with the other man. Cris dove deeper and saw some flashes of the ship's flight deck. The other man was plotting a course. He was joking with the captain. There was a sense of homesickness.

Cris pulled back. He tried to make sense of what he had seen and felt. *The ship's Navigator, maybe?*

The two men continued to talk for three more minutes and then parted ways. The other man carried a duffle bag as he walked away.

Did he just resign? This might be my lucky day. Cris walked up to the captain of the cargo freighter, trying to be unassuming. It proved harder than expected. "Excuse me, sir?"

The captain pivoted around to look at Cris. When he saw who had spoken, he rolled his eyes. "Fok, this is all I need. What do you want, kid?"

Cris was shocked by the tone, after the deference he had been given his whole life. *Remember, you're not that person anymore.* "I was hoping to buy myself a ride aboard your ship."

"We're not a passenger vessel." His annoyance was apparent.

"I can pay—"

"We're not a passenger vessel," the captain repeated.

Fine, then I'll put my education to use. "What about openings on your crew?"

The captain didn't respond at first. His eyes narrowed. "Not unless you know long-range navigation."

"I do." It is the family business, after all.

The captain smirked. "Right."

Cris looked the captain in the eye. "Let me prove it."

The captain scratched his stubble. He sighed. "All right, I'll give you a chance. What's your name?"

Cris was about to respond, but stopped himself, knowing he couldn't let anyone know his true lineage. "Cris Sights."

"I'm Thom Caleri, and this is the *Exler*," the captain said, gesturing to his ship. "Let's go to the flight deck and I'll see if you're full of yourself."

Cris smiled with trained charm and followed Thom onto the ship. The *Exler* was a small freighter compared to many. Built exclusively for space travel, it was long and boxy with a forked backend for the jump drive and a protrusion at the top for the flight deck and living quarters. It was to this upper deck that the gangway led; as with standard freighters, cargo would be offloaded to smaller transport shuttles using a bay in the belly of the ship.

Inside, the *Exler* matched its captain. There were scuff marks along the walls and some deck plates were missing the occasional screw, but the bones were solid. The flight deck was at the end of a short hallway leading from the gangway entrance. It was a cramped room with only two seats. An expansive window spanned the far wall, giving a partial view of the space station and surrounding ships. Most of the controls looked to be physical buttons and switches. However, there was a horizontal touchscreen at the center of the room between the seats, supported by a console marked with the same SiNavTech logo found on all navigation systems.

"Have at it," Thom said, pointing to the touchscreen.

Cris glanced at the branding on the navigation console beneath the screen and noticed it was an older model from around the time he was born. The interface would be slightly different, but the underlying firmware would be identical to the modern systems he had studied.

Cris tapped the touchscreen and it illuminated. A holographic spatial map hovered just above the screen's surface. "Where to?"

"Gallos system," Thom instructed.

Not exactly a tourist destination, but I'll take anywhere other than here. "Okay." Cris went through the time-consuming navigation programming sequence with expert precision, identifying an optimized route for the subspace jump that would take them on a direct course to the destination. He ran four different scenarios and after half an hour settled on a beacon sequence that would allow access to several space stations during the required jump drive cooldown stops along the way. He tested the course with a dummy lock to the first beacon, and it verified his route. "This is my recommendation. Transit time will be eleven days, including the cooldown times for the jump drive."

Thom had watched him closely at every step. A navigation

system was a sensitive piece of equipment for a stranger to access, but there was no other way to vet a new Navigator. "That looks right to me. Except add a few days to the time estimate to account for longer stops so we can sleep."

"I'm happy to change the stopovers if you'd prefer—"

"No, the locations are fine. You did everything correctly." Thom crossed his arms. "I'm just surprised someone your age has experience with course plotting. You can't be much older than what, sixteen?"

"Is that a problem?"

The captain looked pensive. "I suppose not. That's legal age for crew work."

"Does that mean I have the job?"

The captain smiled amiably. "Shite, why not? Some company would be better than none. You can be my Navigation Officer for the trip to Gallos—for starters—in exchange for room and board. If it works out, we can negotiate a salary for the next run."

It's more than a little ironic I'd end up working as a Navigator after being groomed as an heir to SiNavTech. "That's a reasonable offer. I accept."

Thom nodded. "Good." He looked Cris over again. "I have three rules. First, no stealing from me or other members of the crew. Second, no picking fights. And lastly, I won't ask you prying questions if you don't ask them of me."

That last one works to my advantage. "Agreed."

The captain turned the palm of his right hand upward in greeting, the Taran custom for new acquaintances who had not yet earned the trust of physical contact. "Welcome to the *Exler*."

◄ CHAPTER 3 ►

Amazed by his good fortune, Cris accompanied Thom from the flight deck into the belly of the *Exler*. The captain introduced him to the two other crew members, Dom and Neal—both thick, muscled men in their thirties who were responsible for the cargo hold—and gave him a tour of the ship. There was little to see beyond the cargo area, workout room, kitchen and common washroom. Though it was simply appointed and lacked many of the comforts Cris had grown up with on Tararia, the *Exler* was clean enough and mechanically well-maintained from what he could tell.

The last stop in the tour was Cris' new quarters. It was a tiny room with only a bunk, toilet, sink and storage locker. Cris smiled politely when he saw the space, and Thom left him to get settled in. When he was alone, Cris set down his bag and looked around the modest accommodations. *I need to reset my expectations.*

He sat down on the bunk to test it. The mattress was firmer than he would prefer, but it was sufficient. *I wanted to see what life was really like outside the Sietinen estate. It doesn't get more authentic than this.* He took a deep breath. *My entire life is changing.*

He gave himself a few minutes to clear his head and then made his way up to the flight deck. Thom was waiting for him. "Ready to head out?" Cris asked.

"Yes. All stocked and ready to get underway," Thom confirmed.

Cris brought up the saved beacon sequence he had plotted during his interview and set it as the active course in the navigation computer. He locked in the first segment of the trip, a series of five beacons. "All set."

Thom smiled. "Let's go." He strapped into his chair and triggered buttons and switches at the front of the flight deck. A holographic control interface illuminated over the front panels. Using a combination of the holographic display and buttons beneath, Thom undocked the *Exler* and used thrusters to direct the ship away from the space station.

Anticipation swelled in Cris' chest. *I'm leaving for real.*

When the space station orbiting Tararia was a distant speck, Thom activated the jump drive.

A hum filled the air as the drive charged. The entire ship began to vibrate, rattling every rivet. It felt like the ship was going to fall apart, but Cris tried to hide his worry. As the vibration crescendoed, a shifting blue-green aura formed around the ship. It grew steadily brighter and more solid, drawing the ship inward. For a moment, time elongated. The ship slipped into subspace.

Cris let out a slow breath as the rattling subsided. The view through the front window was nothing but shifting blue-green light.

"It's beautiful, isn't it?" Thom said.

"It really is." Cris had taken previous trips via subspace, but the mode of travel was still a novel experience. Even more rarely had he been able to look outside while in transit. *I could get used to this.*

The first sequence of beacons would take several hours to traverse. Cris and Thom settled in for the journey, keeping a casual eye on the navigation beacon locks to make sure they stayed on course. It was uncomfortably quiet.

As much as Cris wanted to be social, he knew his background was very different from Thom's. He had little way of knowing what might give him away as High Dynasty. *What's a safe topic?*

Silence was the safest option, but Cris' lack of sleep from his midnight escape began to catch up with him. He knew he needed some conversation or he wouldn't make it through the rest of the jump.

"So, Thom," Cris said, breaking the silence, "what's the craziest cargo you've ever had to transport? If it's not something confidential."

Thom smiled. "A herd of horses."

"Horses, really?"

The captain nodded. "I imagine you haven't been out to the far colonies. Some worlds that have taken a more agrarian approach to life. They prefer horses to hoverscooters."

"Go figure."

Thom chuckled. "It was messy business. Sweet animals, but I'll take a depleted power cell over a pile of manure any day."

Cris laughed. "I'm with you."

"That was a long time ago." Thom leaned back in his chair. "I now make it a point to steer away from any cargo that isn't inanimate and doesn't fit neatly into a crate."

Thank the stars! I think I would have needed to find another ship. "A valid approach."

"I've been doing lots of textiles transportation for Baellas recently."

Clothing and home furnishings weren't the most grand of the High Dynastic ventures, but important nonetheless. "Is that what we have onboard now?"

"Yes, but I'm ready to switch things up after completing this delivery."

"What do you have in mind?" Cris asked.

"I heard about some new food distribution contracts with

Makaris Corp in the outer colonies. It'd be steady work for several months at a time. I don't particularly love it out there, but can't argue with the pay."

Cris nodded. "That does sound like good, steady work." Food and water filters were a necessity everywhere. Makaris' rank as the third most powerful Dynasty was only constrained by the reliance on SiNavTech's navigation network and VComm for communications.

"I've learned that it all comes down to the specific contract terms. It doesn't really matter what the cargo is when it's all packaged up. In the end, all of the Big 6 are pretty much the same to work for."

Cris' brow furrowed in spite of himself.

Thom must have noticed Cris' confusion. "The six High Dynasties," he clarified.

"Oh, thanks," Cris said as casually as he could. "Haven't heard that before." *So they call us "the Big 6," huh?*

"I had already pegged you for the inner colonies, but that confirms it."

"Tararia itself, actually." Cris regretted the statement the moment he spoke.

The captain nodded. "I'm not surprised. Well, out here, you'll hear a lot of different opinions about the Big 6. Generally speaking, the farther out you go, the less favorable they will become."

"Interesting." *I'll have to watch what I say.*

"Don't get me wrong," Thom continued. "Tarans in aggregate recognize the importance of the core services the Big 6 provide, but most worlds try to have their own identity. The descendants of the older colonies even look and sound different—an entirely divergent race from a native Tararian like yourself. To them, the High Dynasties and the Priesthood feel like very distant, disconnected, and often inconvenient overlords."

But without those services fulfilled by the High Dynasties' companies, everything would fall apart. "I could see that."

"Since the outer colonies try to make it on their own as much as possible, they sometimes get neglected by the central oligarchy. It's one of the reasons I was looking to pick up those Makaris contracts."

"That's good of you." *My instruction always made it sound like it was equal access and opportunity for all the colonies. Maybe that's not the case.*

"Well, first we have to offload this Baellas shipment. Need to take it one contract at a time."

Cris smiled. "Of course."

Thom sat up straight. "Hey, do you know how to play Fastara?"

Cris hesitated. *What in the stars is Fastara?* "I can't say I do."

"Hold on." Thom searched through a cabinet near his seat and produced a deck of plastic playing cards. He removed them from their clear box and fanned them out. There were a series of symbols in different colors on the cards. "I'll teach you. There's no better way to pass the time out here."

"Sounds great."

Thom deactivated the holographic course projection from the navigation console and moved the most vital information to a heads-up display over the front window. The touchscreen top of the console became a perfect tabletop for laying out the game.

"The objective is to win," Thom said with a toothy grin.

Thom went over a series of rules that Cris tried his best to follow. There were a lot of contingencies based on the specific cards in play. After a few confusing explanation attempts, Thom dealt out the first game and walked Cris through an open-hand demonstration. Even with the coaching, Thom won by a ridiculous margin. They played three more rounds in the same manner before switching over to private hands. Cris was still terrible at the game, but he started to understand the mechanics.

While reading Thom's mind would have been an easy solution, it would defeat the purpose of the game—and, that kind of invasion was no way to begin a friendship.

The hours sped by with the rounds of Fastara. Cris was startled when the navigation system flashed, indicating their approach to the exit beacon in the sequence. They cleared the game and moved the display back to the center console.

With a shudder, the ship dropped back into normal space. The swirling blue-green dissipated and they were once again surrounded by blackness and stars.

Cris looked at the map. It was officially the farthest he had ever been from home. "Jump complete." *They'll have a hard time finding me now.*

"Now we take a break," Thom said as he got up from his chair. "The jump drive only needs four hours to cool down, but we'll stay here for eight so we can get some sleep. After this, we'll do two jumps in a day."

"That works for me." Cris got up from his seat, feeling stiff after remaining stationary for so long. "Hey... Thank you for the job."

"Everyone deserves the chance to start a new life," Thom said. "Get some rest."

Cris went to his room and got into bed. The ship's engines produced the perfect background hum to lull Cris to sleep. *I'm free.*

<>

An alarm sounded, echoing through the tiny metal room. Cris' eyes shot open. A red light strobed above his door. *Stars! What's going on?*

He rolled off his bed, clutching his ears to muffle the alarm. *Are we under attack?* The metal deck plates felt like ice under his bare feet. Wearing only pajama pants and a t-shirt, he stumbled toward the door. Something didn't feel right.

Cris' stomach turned over. He tried to take a step and couldn't get traction. Slowly, he lifted off the ground. *The artificial gravity is shut off! Shite!* He continued to drift upward as he struggled. An acidic burn filled the back of his throat, a combination of nerves and the weightlessness. *I'm going to be sick.* He grasped at the walls and managed to propel himself toward the toilet in the corner. No sooner had he raised the lid then his stomach emptied. He coughed and spat for a moment, only to be horrified to see the vomit rising upward without gravity to hold it down. He slammed the lid down to trap the contents in the toilet bowl.

Still feeling queasy, he gripped the wall and shimmied himself back toward the door. He hit the release to slide it open.

Red light strobed in the hallway, casting eerie shadows across the riveted planes. Cris' heart raced. *Where is everyone? Are we going to die?* His heart pounded in his ears. The taste of sick still in his mouth made him want to hurl again. He tried to suppress the feeling as he gripped the bulkhead outside his door to move toward the flight deck.

"Thom!" No reply. Cris inched along the wall, afraid to let go. He couldn't hear anything over the deafening alarm and the pounding in his ears. "Thom, where are you?"

Cris made it to the gym and opened the door. Empty. He knocked on the doors to Dom and Neal's rooms, but there was no reply. He kept pushing forward. As he approached the kitchen, the door slid open.

Inside, the three other members of the crew were floating comfortably in midair. Thom was grinning and Dom and Neal were laughing hysterically.

Cris stared at them in shock. "What…?"

Thom laughed at Cris' bewildered expression. "You didn't think you could come onboard without a little hazing, did you?"

Cris felt his face flush. "So there isn't an emergency."

"Not at all." Thom hit a button on the wall and the alarm

silenced, though the red flashing light remained. "However, I am pleased to report that all emergency systems are functioning perfectly."

Bomax. Cris steadied himself against the doorframe, his ears still ringing from the alarm. "Well played."

"So sullen! It was all in good fun," Thom said.

Right. "Now can you restore the gravity? I feel like I'm going to puke again."

Dom and Neal burst into another round of laughter.

Thom looked slightly apologetic. "Again? You planet-lovers never fare so well at first. Cleaning supplies are in the cabinet over here, if you need anything."

No more servants to pick up after me. "Thanks. I think most of it was... contained."

"Well, let's get you back on your feet." The captain glided toward the door.

Cris eased out of the way so Thom could get by, and then followed him through the hall toward the darkened flight deck.

Thom pulled himself into the pilot's seat. Even in the challenging light of the red strobe, he easily manipulated the buttons and switches on the control panel. "This is why we have physical buttons rather than exclusively touchscreen interfaces," he said. "You can run on backup batteries for days this way. Holographics are a massive power drain. And difficult to control in zero-G."

"Ah, I was wondering." *I can't believe they messed with me like that.*

The red light was replaced by the normal soft yellow ambiance. Simultaneously, Cris felt himself drawn toward the floor, and he repositioned accordingly. He breathed a deep sigh of relief as his bare feet made contact with the ground once more. His stomach settled. "That's better." *I hope I'm cut out for life in space.*

Thom beamed. "Congratulations. You've been officially

inducted."

Yay. "I'm going back to bed." He heard Thom chuckling in the flight deck all the way back to his room.

◄ CHAPTER 4 ►

Over the next several days, Cris embraced his place in the *Exler*'s crew and set aside thoughts of his old life. By sheer will, he fell into the ways of space and vowed to leave behind his former existence. He spent long hours in the flight deck with Thom, hanging on every word of the captain's stories. As Thom promised, Cris was never asked intrusive questions and he never pressed Thom.

His daily activities were nothing like his schooling on Tararia, and Cris relished the change. By ship's day, he kept Thom company in the flight deck while they traversed the vast network connecting the star systems. It was the first real contact Cris had ever had with the impressive SiNavTech infrastructure, and he couldn't help but feel pride for what his family had built over the generations.

As the days stretched on, Cris incrementally improved his skills with Fastara. He could only win one in twenty games against Thom—if the captain got a particularly bad draw—but it was progress. Ultimately, the win rate didn't matter; life was good if the biggest decision he had to make was regarding which card to play.

The jumps toward Gallos grew monotonous. By the end, Cris was ready to see more than the four rooms where he'd spent the majority of his time for the last two weeks. Though some of their stopovers were near space stations, Thom insisted it wasn't worth the docking fees to berth. They were confined to the *Exler* until they reached their destination.

The final jumps went by quickly, knowing they were nearing the end. When they dropped out of subspace after the last jump, Cris' heart leaped with excitement as he glimpsed the distant outline of a sprawling space station. *Gallos. Finally.*

He had learned from Thom that the Gallos System was a commercial hub for the surrounding colonies. Its central space station dwarfed even the massive port at Tararia. There were rambling offshoots in every direction, seemingly constructed to meet ad hoc demands for expansion over the years. The result was a daunting labyrinth of corridors and gangways where Cris imagined a person could get lost and never be seen again. He gulped.

"We have a docking reservation where our client is meeting us," Thom stated. "I'll go to the Makaris field office later today to talk about a distribution contract."

"What should I do?" Cris asked.

Thom rubbed his chin. "Are you interested in staying on with me?"

He's been good to me, even if it's been a little boring at times. I can't imagine a much better setup. Cris nodded. "If you'll have me."

"I can offer you continued room and board, plus five percent of my profits."

That's probably a terrible deal, but I don't need the money. "That works."

Thom seemed surprised. "Okay, well good. You've been great company. It'll be nice having you around."

I guess that really makes me an official member of the crew. "Do you want me to come with you to the Makaris meeting?"

"No, best leave that to me. Take some time to wander around and enjoy yourself. We'll head out in a couple of days."

They finished docking with the station and Cris was soon

left to fend for himself. He took some time to shower in the shared washroom and change into clean clothes before venturing from the *Exler*.

The space station was a completely different environment than the port at Tararia. It was immediately apparent that the pace was slower, with individuals and small groups strolling as they talked business or caught up on personal lives. Cris found it easy to walk off the *Exler* and wander down the corridor without coming close to anyone else.

At first, he couldn't resist sneaking a few telepathic probes on the passersby. Most minds were preoccupied with business dealings or the other mundane aspects of life. He was tempted to look deeper and stretch the skills he kept in check around his friends, but he held back. *It's not polite to pry, friend or not.*

And while telepathy was a practical skill, what he really desired was to learn telekinesis. Thus far, all of his attempts at object levitation had been non-starters. He knew he needed instruction, and a spaceport in the outer territories might be his best bet to find a teacher to get him started. As much as he'd like to join the TSS and get official training, reaching out to them would give away his position to Tararian authorities—granting him a one-way ticket on a transport back home. Keeping a low profile was his safest option, even if it meant taking longer to reach his goals.

As he made his way down the hallway, foot traffic slowly picked up. After a short while, he found himself at an intersection with what appeared to be a central mall. Shops lined the broad corridor, with merchants barking their wares.

There were significantly more people in the shopping district compared to the docking area near the *Exler*. People with every variety of skin tone and feature, dressed in all manner of clothing styles, were going about their business. The hum of conversation filled the space, making it feel lively without being frantic.

Now this is what I had imagined. Cris looked around in wonder. The colorful storefronts with illuminated signs and attention-grabbing holographic gimmicks stretched on for as far as he could see in both directions, broken up only by other side corridors to the various docking wings. *There's so much to explore!* He made note of the shops near the *Exler*'s docking location so he could find his way back, then arbitrarily set off down the mall to his right.

As he strolled, there was a slow change in his surroundings—so subtle that he didn't notice at first. The vibrant colors and flashy ads gave way to metal signs with static typography. The wording on most of these signs was vague, such as "Sundries from far and wide" or "Trade, Barter and Pawn." The people also changed. Though still covering the spectrum of physical traits, their clothing was more worn and they appeared to be constantly evaluating the value of everything they surveyed.

Cris was so taken in by the freedom to wander on his own that he didn't realize he was growing increasingly anxious under the scrutinizing gaze of the shopkeepers and their patrons. When he finally became aware of his surroundings, he realized he stood out from the few people left roaming the corridor. *Maybe it's time to get out of sight for a while and do some shopping.*

One of the shops off to Cris' left caught his eye. The printed sign boasted discount ships and parts. *How discounted? Maybe I could buy my own ship one day and have real autonomy.* He decided to investigate.

The entrance to the shop was an open doorway two meters wide. Inside, on both walls of the shop, tiered shelving rose to the three-meter-high ceiling. Other shelves were positioned perpendicular to the wall, forming a maze of forgotten artifacts. Random ship parts were nearly overflowing from the shelves, and some larger items rested on the floor. The disorganization and compact layout were unappealing, but Cris was too intrigued by the dream of eventually having his own ship to care.

The perpendicular offshoots from the shelves prevented a direct view deeper into the store. With no proprietor in sight, Cris headed toward the back. He weaved through the shelves until he came to an open area.

A young woman was lounging on a metal counter, her long legs crossed with one of her booted feet bobbing in the air. She looked to be a few years older than Cris, and had dark hair with fuchsia highlights that was pulled up into a sloppy ponytail. Long bangs fell over her maple eyes. When Cris approached, she looked up. She appraised him and smiled. "Well, hello there." She slid off the counter.

"Hi," Cris replied. "Do you work here?"

"I do." She looked Cris over again. "What can I do for you?" She shifted her weight to one hip and stood akimbo. Though she was fairly tall and thin, her revealing clothing emphasized every curve.

Cris tried to keep his eyes on her face. "I saw on your sign that you have ships for sale."

She nodded. "That's right. In the market for anything in particular?"

"Just browsing for now. How much for a basic craft with a jump drive?"

"Well, let's take a look at our inventory." The woman sauntered around to the back side of the counter and grabbed a tablet from underneath. She placed the tablet on the counter and activated a holographic projection of the inventory list, which included images of the crafts and some basic features. She drummed her fingers on the counter. "Need room for passengers? Traveling with anyone?"

"Not really. Just me." Cris looked around the equipment in the shop. Some of it was worn, but much of it appeared to be almost brand new.

"Okay, let's see…" After flicking through the list of ships, the woman selected one and brought up a more detailed display on the projector. "This would be your best bet. For something entry-level."

The ship was only ten meters long and had the aerodynamic look of a craft designed for atmospheric entry. While it would be functional, Cris doubted he could stay sane in such a small space for any prolonged period of time. "How much?"

"76,000 credits."

There's no way I could spend that much without drawing suspicion. "Not bad, but it's a little more than I was hoping to spend."

The woman shrugged. "Well, you're paying for the scrubbed ID, of course."

"Of course." *Stars! These are ships for smuggling.* He realized with dismay that the new equipment around him was likely scrap from stolen vessels.

"How would you pay?" the woman asked. "We might be able to work out a deal."

The discomfort that had been pestering the back of Cris' mind since he entered the shop washed over him full-force—a wave of ill intent that now seemed impossible to have missed before. "Really, I—"

He was cut off by the woman turning to yell deeper into the store. "Merl! We have a customer."

The sound of creaking metal drew Cris' attention to his side. A man with arms nearly the size of Cris' torso emerged from a hidden doorway, blocking the exit path.

Simultaneously, Merl emerged from a back room behind the counter. He was two heads taller than Cris, all muscle, and had geometric tattoos on the side of his face and going up his bare arms. With his eyes fixed on Cris, he approached the counter. He put an arm around his slight companion. "Oh, Danni, you got us a good one."

"He's pretty, isn't he?" Danni said. "Traveling alone. And he comes with a nice bank account."

Shite! This is bad. Warnings flashed in Cris' mind, sending a chill down his spine. *I don't think they just smuggle ship parts…*

"How much do you think we could get for him?" Danni asked Merl.

"Looks like good breeding," Merl replied, evaluating Cris. "Probably at least 50,000 credits to the right buyer."

The man from the side room took a step toward Cris.

Run! Cris bolted, ducking past the towering man who had come to block him in. He felt the breeze from the man's arms trying to grab him, but managed to make it through. After tearing around the maze of shelves, he ran full speed as soon as he was in the open corridor. He didn't slow until he was again surrounded by lively merchants and bright ads.

Cris stepped off to the side of the hall. He leaned forward, hands resting on his thigh—shaking and his breath ragged. He found an open stretch of wall to lean against. *I should have seen that coming.* Reading everyone's minds might not be polite, but perhaps some way necessary to protect himself.

He took a couple minutes to calm his breathing and racing heart. Despite his excitement from earlier, when he looked out at the crowd again, he felt like everyone in the port was staring at him suspiciously. *I think I need a break.*

The *Exler* seemed like the only safe place. He took a direct route back, thankful he had paid attention to the docking location. When he made it to the ship, he was about to go into his room when he saw that Thom was in the flight deck. He continued down the hall and poked his head in. "Hi Thom."

The captain looked up with surprise. "Back already? I figured you'd be partying all night."

Cris collapsed into his Navigator's chair. "It was a lot to take in at once. I think I'll just turn in early."

Thom raised an eyebrow. "Everything okay?"

"Yeah, just… acclimating." *Probably best if he doesn't know how inexperienced I really am. There's no way I'm traveling alone any time soon.*

Thom nodded. "Yes, it's quite different out here than around Tararia."

I'll say… Cris sighed inwardly.

"And even more so in the outer colonies where we're headed."

Where we're headed? Cris perked up. "Wait, you got the Makaris contract?"

Thom smiled. "I did—and a good one. Fifteen months, with scheduled stops on a service route. We'll have supply pickups every two weeks at stations, so you'll have plenty of time to get used to everything."

"Perfect." *All this will start feeling normal eventually, right?*

"I got us a little something to celebrate." Thom pulled out two small glasses and a bottle of a dark brown liquid from the cabinet by his chair. "I know you're not quite of age, but one drink won't hurt you." He filled the glasses and passed one to Cris.

Stars! It would be rude to turn him down. Cris took the glass. *Besides, I could use a drink.*

Thom downed the contents of his glass in one gulp.

Cris took a cautious whiff of the liquid. It seemed more like a cleaning supply than anything fit for a person to consume. *Here it goes.* He took the full glass into his mouth and swallowed. It burned all the way down and left his stomach feeling warm. He coughed a couple of times, feeling the burn up in his sinuses. "Wow, that's…"

"That's real liquor. Not like those 'liqueurs' and sparkling shite everyone drinks back in the central worlds."

Everyone drinks those because they actually taste good. "I appreciate the introduction to the real stuff." *And now I know what to avoid as much as possible.*

"It'll knock you on your ass if you're not careful." Thom poured himself another glass and offered Cris some more.

Cris hastily declined. "I'm sure it can." Without warning, he started to feel a little light-headed and tingly. *This stuff acts fast.* "I think it's bedtime for me."

Thom seemed disappointed. "All right. Sleep well."

Cris rose. "Thanks for the drink." *And thank you for taking me in.*

<> <> <>

The news was not what TSS High Commander Jason Banks had hoped to hear. "What do you mean he's 'gone'?"

Agent Jarek's image on the viewscreen, almost indistinguishable from real life, looked uncomfortable. "His parents didn't want to talk to us. We were able to glean that he slipped out in the middle of the night a couple of weeks ago."

Shite! We should have been keeping a closer watch. "We need to find him. As soon as possible."

Jarek frowned. "He could be anywhere, sir. We checked all the registries for passenger ships, but there was nothing. If he's on a cargo freighter, there are hundreds of possibilities, multiplied exponentially by transfers at another port. I think we need to wait it out until we get some kind of lead."

Banks rubbed his eyes under his tinted glasses. *This is a disaster.* "Fine. Make some contacts out there to keep watch for us. We'll wait it out." *Let's hope we find him before the Priesthood does. I don't want to risk a repeat of last time.*

PART 2: AWAKENING

◄ CHAPTER 5 ►

"Game." Cris laid down his victorious hand of Fastara.

Thom threw down his cards in disgust. "That's five in a row. I've created a monster."

"Oh, come on now. Be a good sport."

"Constant loss kind of takes the fun out of it."

Right, like it was awesome for me when we first started playing. "You had a good run. This was bound to happen eventually. After all, I have had a year of daily practice." Cris grinned. He knew he had just been lucky with his last several draws—he and Thom were equal in their playing ability, despite the recent winning streak. *I can't resist getting in a few jabs while I can.*

They were nearing the end of another delivery cycle on their Makaris contract. After only ten months with Thom, Cris could hardly believe he'd ever had any other life. Since his initial mishaps, he had become comfortable with the customs of nomadic space life. With dozens of stopovers in space stations, he had learned how to identify the good areas from the bad, and he was proficient at using covert telepathic probes when needed.

To his relief, the food distribution work offered far more variety than the initial, dull trip to Gallos. They traveled for no more than two days at a time without making a stop to offload, which helped the time pass.

Privately, Cris had kept up with his studies and physical

training in the *Exler*'s small gym, not wanting his skills to atrophy; however, it was because he enjoyed it, rather than feeling like it was something he had to do. He kept steady watch for news about his parents back in Sieten, but heard little. There was never an announcement about his disappearance—that would have been a disastrous political move—but he figured there must be private detectives looking for him. The prospect was disconcerting, but he tried to feel confident in his ability to remain undetectable. He was the Navigator for a cargo freighter, and as far as anyone else was concerned, he was born to fulfill such a duty.

The navigation system beeped. They had reached the last beacon in the sequence.

Thom jumped at the chance to clear the cards from their play surface. "Thank the stars! I need some time away from the onslaught."

Cris shook his head and laughed. *He'll get over it.* He checked the lock on the exit beacon; it was solid. "Aldria, here we come."

The *Exler* dropped out of subspace. Ahead of them, in the distance, was one of the smaller stations in the sector. They had previously been there four times on their delivery rounds. Unlike many other stations, Aldria was predominantly a stopover for merchants, rather than serving as a residence for any sizable population.

They went through the docking protocol with the remote attendant. As soon as the clamps were in place, Thom rose from his seat. "I'll handle the offloading. Go get some of that fried thing you like so much."

Because it's delicious! "Best in the outer colonies."

"So you've told me every time since we first came here." Thom shooed Cris away with his hand. "Now go, before I change my mind."

Cris eagerly complied. There were few things he missed

from his home, but fried leeca was one. It was common street food on Tararia, but the Sietinen family chef had made it for him one time and he was instantly hooked. He had stumbled across a vendor in the Aldria Station on their first stopover and was thrilled to discover that the rendition thoroughly lived up to his memory.

The vendor was on the opposite side of the station. Cris took his time taking in the sights, happy to stretch his legs in a manner other than on a treadmill. They stopped at stations frequently enough, but rarely was he afforded free time to idly gaze at wares.

Even after a year of travel, he was still amazed by the quantity and breadth of products available in ports. There was a gadget to fulfill every need—both real needs, and those invented strictly for the sake of sales. It was difficult to imagine all of the inventory selling, yet the system perpetuated itself. Cris was struck by the scale of it. *I'm only here at this one moment. How many millions of people pass by just out of sight in space every day?* Thinking in those terms put his own miniscule existence in perspective. *But I'm not no one, as much as I try to blend in. Even with all those countless people, most would still know my birth name. That recognition means something.* It was humbling.

Cris took a wrong turn at first, but eventually found the fried leeca vendor's red cart. A rich scent of frying dough wafted down the hall. The cart was a freestanding box a couple meters square and just tall enough to stand inside, with a half-open wall to the front. Its crimson color made Cris think of his favorite flower patch in the Sietinen estate's gardens. He beamed at the proprietor as he approached.

She was a sturdy woman of middle years, named Roselyn based on the credentials displayed in front of her cart. There was a warmth to her that reminded Cris of the nanny who had cared for him until he was six. She tilted her head and gave Cris a slight smile in return. There was a hint of recognition in her burnt umber eyes. "You're back."

She remembers me? I guess I couldn't stay completely anonymous forever. "I could never pass up the opportunity to get a taste of home."

"It's been almost two months, hasn't it?" Roselyn asked as she rotated the contents of the basket in her fryer within the cart.

Cris nodded. "Yes, sadly. Our rounds only bring us here every nine weeks."

Roselyn frowned. "What a shame. I've missed that adorable smile of yours." She winked at him.

Stars! Is she flirting with me? He smiled politely and took half a step back. "I'll take two orders, please."

"Absolutely. I'll have a fresh batch ready in a couple minutes." She flipped the contents of the basket again.

"I've been looking forward to it all week."

Roselyn inclined her head. "You flatter me. Are you here for long?"

"Just for a few hours to pick up our cargo, then on to Elarine," Cris replied with a dour expression. *My least favorite of all the ports.*

"Elarine…" The vendor's brow furrowed. "I've heard of it, but never been."

"Don't bother. There's nothing to see. It's small and unremarkable in every way."

Roselyn grinned. "Looking forward to your visit, then?"

"Can't wait…"

"Well, I hope this makes it easier for you." Roselyn removed the basket from the fryer and placed six fried patties onto a plastic plate. The golden dough of the leeca was still sizzling. She set the plate on a ledge atop the front opening to her cart. "Four credits."

Cris pulled the physical currency chips out of his pocket and gave her five credits. Electronic transfers were far more common, but he feared the faked credentials on his alias bank account wouldn't hold up to thorough scrutiny. As a precaution, he had adopted the practice of using chips instead.

He blew on a piece of leeca to cool it and took a bite—warm and savory with just the right touch of sweetness. It brought him back to his early life, before preparing for his future responsibilities became the sole focus. *I did have this as a kid. I guess it wasn't all bad.* "It's excellent," he said while still chewing.

"Enjoy," Roselyn said. "Have fun in Elarine."

Hah. "Thanks." He waved goodbye and began wandering back toward the *Exler*.

Cris finished up the leeca while casually strolling through the port, reflecting on some of the good times from his childhood on Tararia. He wandered by some shops and looked at completely impractical, unnecessary items. As he browsed, he even noticed oversized pulse guns that couldn't possibly be legal and some openly displayed narcotics. *It really is different out here.*

With romanticized thoughts of Tararia still floating through his mind, Cris was on his final approach to the *Exler* when he happened to overhear the Sietinen name mentioned in a conversation. It had been so long since he'd heard the name directly—rather than a generic mention of the Big 6—that it caught him off-guard. He stopped and looked around to identify who was talking. After a moment, he spotted two merchants drinking at a walk-up bar. Curious, Cris walked over so he could hear the details.

"You're right, the entire government system is corrupt," the first merchant was saying. "Regardless of what the highest Dynasties like Sietinen and Vaenetri say, the Priesthood runs the show." He took a sip of a green liquid from his glass. "But it doesn't matter who's in charge. Nothing happening in the outside worlds matters to any of them."

Cris had heard numerous similar conversations over the last year. Each one was a series of unflattering generalizations about the High Dynasties and how no individual could possibly ever care. He was sick of hearing it. *We're not all like that. I'm different. The Priesthood is the real menace, not the Dynasties.* He was about to walk away.

"Real conflict is headed our way, but they do nothing," the other merchant said. "I've been to the outermost territories recently. It's brutal, and it's only getting worse."

Cris hung back. *That's new…*

"They're certainly not going to tell us what's going on out there," the first merchant agreed. "Meanwhile, countless people are starving and being taxed to death."

"No shite. All of those purists think alike. It's about maintaining power and getting richer, not helping people."

"Thank the stars for the TSS! I hear at least they have the decency to tell their first-year trainees about some of what's going on in the rest of the galaxy. Give people a chance to get out of whatever hole they were born into."

"It's hardly enough. We're all foked."

The first merchant gulped the rest of his glass. The second did likewise.

What kind of conflict are they talking about? Cris knew it wasn't his place to intrude, but he was feeling inspired after his recent reflections on Tararia. He stepped up to the merchants. "The High Dynasties do care about their people. You shouldn't be so dismissive."

The merchants stared at him, taken by surprise. Both burst into uproarious laughter.

"How naïve!" the first merchant exclaimed. "Generation after generation it's always the same shite. They ignore us out here, and that's never going to change."

"There is always hope for change," Cris countered.

The merchant scoffed. "Hope, maybe, but that doesn't mean

it will ever happen. The Dynasties and Priesthood control everything, and we're nothing to them. You or I can't do anything about that." He turned back to his companion with an indifferent smile, shaking his head.

Perhaps there isn't anything he can do, but I am in a unique position. "Then someone already high up has to bring about change," Cris said with renewed vigor. "Someone who doesn't share their predecessors' ideals."

The merchants shook their heads, laughed again as they turned to face Cris.

"You're still here?" the second merchant jeered as his drink was refreshed by the bartender.

The first merchant sighed. "The problem *is* the people with influence! Everyone has been born into their position, and no one would give that up."

I would. There have to be others. "The Dynasties are only as powerful as the people let them be."

"If that's the case," said the second merchant, "then the Dynasties are doing a foking good job of keeping the populace placated through lies."

Some passersby took notice of the debate and stopped to listen.

We don't lie to anyone. "I'm sure people are told what they need to know."

The merchant's expression became completely serious. "What about a war? Is it right to keep the war a secret?"

What war? Cris hesitated. "Someone thinks so." *Have they kept secrets even from me?*

The merchant shrugged and waved his hand, brushing Cris off. He tried to crack a smile. "Then what does it matter? Whether it's the Priesthood or someone new, it'd still come down to one group deciding what others should know."

Could there really be a conflict going on that I don't know about? "But what if it really is for the best? Knowledge and power often come with a price. Perhaps it is necessary for a few to bear the burden."

A murmur of agreement passed through the small crowd watching the discussion.

What does he know about the war? Cris was about to reach out to the merchant's mind to see what he could glean, but a jeer pulled his attention back to the present.

"What do *you* know? You're no one!" The merchant's eyes narrowed as he focused on Cris.

Cris looked around the crowd. "Everyone can do something." *I might not love politics, but maybe I can do what no one else has been willing to do.*

The merchant shook his head. "The Dynasties and the Priesthood have been this way for as far back as anyone can remember. There's no point in talking about change. Anyone who does would likely end up the same way as the Dainetris Dynasty—ruined and all but forgotten. When it comes to matters of Tararia, civilians have no influence."

Cris examined the expectant faces in the crowd. "Then the remaining Dynasties have to listen. With their help, the Priesthood could be brought down."

The merchant recoiled, eyes darting. "Watch what you say— the Priesthood hears everything."

No wonder the Priesthood has so much control. People shy away at its very mention. "I don't fear the Priesthood."

The merchant froze, his gaze fixed on Cris.

Cris looked at the ground. *Stars! What am I doing?* He glanced up, noticing all the people around him looking on with a mixture of wonder and apprehension. *I have to end this.* "I'll be on my way now." He turned away from the merchant. "Excuse me." He pushed his way past the onlookers before the merchant could protest. As he retreated, he thought he saw Thom standing in the crowd.

Cris rushed back to the *Exler*. *Is the Priesthood really*

concealing a war? He went straight to his quarters and sat down on his bunk, his mind spinning. *Who is the enemy? Over what? Why would everyone on Tararia keep it from me? Do they even know...?* Never before had he heard rumors of a war. The occasional spat, surely, but not a war. He tried to rationalize the claim, but got nowhere. After several minutes, he caught himself. *It doesn't matter. I'm trying to forget that life.*

With a deep sigh, Cris forced himself off his bunk. He figured he may as well distract himself by preparing the next route for their upcoming deliveries.

An hour of sporadic work passed in the flight deck. Though some questions still churned in the background, Cris soon felt much more settled. However, he became anxious again when Thom entered, looking concerned.

"What is it, Thom?" Cris asked. *He never looks at me like that.*

The captain shifted uncomfortably on his feet. "I— I was just surprised to hear you say those things at the bar earlier."

Cris dropped his eyes to the floor, thinking back to the encounter with the merchants. "I'm sorry for my behavior, Thom—" *It was so stupid of me to say those things!*

Thom shook his head. "You were just speaking your mind." He took a deep breath. "But, you can't threaten Tararian authorities like that. People can complain and wish things were different, but what you said about bringing down the Priesthood—that's just foolish."

Yet, he must know I'm right—that they're the root of Tararia's problems. "I understand."

"Good." Thom looked around the small room, not meeting Cris' eyes. "Now, can we just move on?" Cris nodded, but Thom still looked distraught when he left the room.

Cris' heart began to race. Something about Thom's demeanor had changed. *Stars, of course! Only someone from a Dynasty would dare speak out against the Priesthood in public...*

and Thom knows it. Shite.

For two days, he and Thom avoided eye contact, but they eventually returned to their normal routine. Still, the encounter with the merchant had moved Cris, and his subliminal thoughts turned to Tararia. He had the power to make a difference—in a way few others could. However, he couldn't bring himself to go back. Yet. He wanted no part of the current political system. But, with the right alliances, perhaps things could change one day. *For now, there is no place for me there. I still have so much to see.*

‹ CHAPTER 6 ›

Cris strolled through the Elarine spaceport, thankful to be on leave from the delivery routine. *Even a stopover at Elarine is better than being cooped up on the* Exler.

The selection of wares in the shops was limited and bland compared to those in the larger ports, but it passed the time. He wandered from shop to shop, keeping to himself. There were few travelers in the corridors, and most of the shopkeepers seemed disinterested until someone wanted to make a purchase.

As Cris came out of one of the establishments, he was startled to see two men watching him from across the hall. They were dressed entirely in black, with tinted glasses and sleek overcoats that hung to their knees—a stark contrast to the colorful merchants. He tensed. Something about them felt unusual.

He shook off the uneasy feeling and headed down the corridor deeper into the port, wanting to distance himself. Out of the corner of his eye, he noticed that the men were heading in his direction.

Who could they be? He thought for a moment. *Stars! Are they my parent's detectives? Bomax, I probably gave myself away in that argument during our last stopover at Aldria.* Pulse racing, Cris abruptly turned around to hurry back toward the *Exler*. To his dismay, the men followed.

I can't let them take me back! Cris broke into a run. He came to the central mall of the port and darted through the crowd, careful to avoid colliding with any of the travelers. When he came to an intersection, he nimbly stepped off to the side and sprinted around a bend in the hall in an attempt to evade the two men. He took a few more turns, but he soon found himself in a dead-end passage. *Shite! Where can I go?*

Cris halted. He was about to wheel around, but in the stillness noticed the pounding of footsteps right behind him.

Before he could turn, Cris was thrown to the ground, tackled from behind. With his arms pinned to his sides in a horrific embrace, he fell forward. Lurching to the side, his shoulder took the hit to avoid smacking his head on the metal deck plates. He rolled to his stomach, weighted down. Someone was on his back. Cris' hands found the floor, and he pushed up, throwing all of his weight sideways to flip his assailant to the ground and crush him against the deck plates. The attacker's grip loosened. Cris jabbed with his elbows and broke free. He scrambled across the hallway.

Cris expected to see one of the two men dressed in black. Instead, he saw a man of average height, robed in brown with his face hidden in the shadow of his hood. Cris recognized the golden symbol hanging from a chain around the man's neck, marking him as an associate of the Priesthood of the Cadicle. *The Priesthood.* Cris suddenly remembered the conversation with his father the afternoon before he left Tararia. *I never did find out why they wanted to meet with me.*

As the Priest recovered on the floor, the two black-clad men emerged from around a bend in the hall. There was a hint of shock on their otherwise stoic faces.

Cris was about to address the men when the Priest leaped to his feet. He pulled out a pulse gun from underneath his robe. "Give me all your valuables."

Trembling and sore, Cris grabbed ten credit chips from his pocket and threw them on the ground. "I have nothing else." It was the truth. His heart pounded in his ears. *Why would a member of the Priesthood be mugging people at a spaceport?*

"Hand over everything you have or die," the Priest threatened.

Cris looked more closely at the figure and caught a brief glimpse of piercing red-brown eyes under the hood. The eyes contained such intense sadness that Cris felt a twinge of sorrow, despite his peril. But, the gaze was also one of complete fear. The gun hummed as it began to charge.

Cris looked back toward the two other men, but they remained at the end of the hall. He was on his own.

The Priest murmured something that Cris couldn't quite make out. He pointed the gun toward Cris' chest.

"No!" Cris held up his hands. *There's no escape.* He felt dizzy, a buzzing in his head. *I don't want to die.*

Undeterred, the robed figure fired.

It should have only taken an infinitesimal moment for the shot to reach him, but the beam halted just beyond the muzzle of the gun. There was no perceivable motion. Cris looked around, seeing the Priest holding the gun and the two people in black observing from a distance. The moment continued. *I can get away.* Cris dove to the side, but didn't fully feel the movement. He was in midair, falling, but he didn't feel connected to himself. Nothing stirred around him. He blinked.

Cris hit the ground hard. There was a flash as the pulse beam struck the empty wall.

The Priest spun to face him, mystified.

Cris could barely breathe. He felt charged, as if filled with electricity. He looked around with wonder—he was in a different place than he had been a moment sooner. *What's going on...?* He shoved his confusion aside as he saw the Priest raising his weapon once more. *This isn't a mugging—it's an assassination!* "Stop!"

As the Priest was about to fire again, Cris held up his hand in what he thought to be a futile act of protection. However, the motion threw the Priest backward against the wall—slamming him into the metal plating with enough force to dent the metal sheeting. He slid into a crumpled heap on the floor.

Cris scrambled to his feet. *Did I just do that? How...?* He turned to the men in black who were still standing motionless at the end of the hall. "Who are you?" he stammered.

Without responding, one of the men walked over to the brown mound on the floor and nudged the Priest with his foot. Cris got a sickening feeling in the pit of his stomach that the Priest was dead, but then saw that he had responded to the nudge. The man backed away, giving the Priest some room.

The robed figure rose unsteadily and looked around, dazed from the impact with the wall. When he caught sight of Cris, he backed away, terror evident in his trembling movement. After a moment, he noticed the two men in black clothing and he froze, apparently recognizing them. His eyes darted between Cris and the men. He said something to Cris, but Cris didn't understand the language. With one more glance at the two black-clad men, the Priest passed them and fled down the hall. He didn't look back.

The man who had nudged the Priest bent down to pick up the pulse gun from the floor. He placed it inside his coat and turned toward Cris.

"Who are you?" Cris repeated, still shaking. He took an unsteady breath. *Why didn't they help me?* He looked the two men over and tried to assess their minds, but found only an impassible void. They appeared to be wary of Cris, but that was understandable after what he had just done. *Stars! What do I do? I can't outrun them.* He took another breath. "Why were you following me?"

"Are you Cristoph Sietinen-Talsari?" the man finally asked.

"That depends. Are you here to kill me, too?"

The two men exchanged looks. "No, we're not here to harm

you," the second man said.

"Did my parents send you to find me?"

"Have you ever done that before?" the first man asked, ignoring his question.

Cris was about to make an indignant remark, but stopped himself. "No." He looked down. "I don't even know what 'that' was." *What's happening to me?*

"No, your parents didn't send us," the other man said after a slight pause, coming to join his colleague. "If you come with us, we can explain everything."

Cris shook his head, finding it increasingly difficult to remain calm. "After what just happened, I'm not in the mood for vague answers. And I'm not going anywhere with people who stood by and did nothing while someone attacked me! Who are you and why are you here?"

The first man nodded to the second. They each pressed their jacket lapel, which activated a projection of their credentials.

Cris examined the holographic images hovering in front of him. His eyes widened. *The TSS!*

"I'm sorry, we're not allowed to intervene in matters regarding the Priesthood. We're with the Tararian Selective Service," the first man said. "I'm Agent Jarek and this is Agent Dodes." He gestured to his partner and then deactivated his ID.

The Priesthood is so powerful that not even the TSS will stand up to them. Cris crossed his arms. "What do you want?"

"The TSS is here on our own accord," Jarek continued. "We were deployed to your family's estate on Tararia to speak with you, only to find that you were missing. Your parents probably have their own people looking for you, but it looks like we found you first. Just in time, it seems—especially considering what you just pulled off without any proper training in telekinesis."

Cris swallowed hard. "And what was 'it'? I have no idea how…" *What if I can't control it? I could hurt someone—Thom, myself... And why does the Priesthood want me dead? Everything was going great. I fit in, I was normal...*

"We're not the best people to answer that," Jarek said.

"Then what do you want from me? You still haven't told me why you're here." *Is there anyone I can trust?*

Agent Jarek studied Cris. "We're here regarding your future."

Cris tensed. "My future?"

"The TSS has been following you with great interest for the past few years," Dodes said. He looked over to Jarek, who nodded. "We would like to extend an invitation for you to train with us."

There was a time when that would have been a dream come true, but now... "I'm not sure what to say."

"I know this comes as a surprise," Jarek responded. "But, the TSS feels you have great potential, which is only evidenced by the abilities you've demonstrated today. I'm sure that our superiors can deal with any reservations you may have. If you'll accompany us to Headquarters, our High Commander can answer your questions." He glanced at the spot where the Priest had been. "And, we can offer you security."

Cris looked down. He might not be so lucky if the Priesthood came after him again. *I still have no idea why they would try to kill me... I don't want to give up the freedom I have now, but I need to learn about these abilities if I want to truly protect myself.* "What would I have to do?"

"Just gather your things and come with us. We have a ship waiting on the other side of the port," Jarek said.

Cris nodded. "The *Exler*'s back this way." *I have absolutely no idea what I'm getting myself into.*

Cris led the way to the *Exler*. He left the Agents at the foot of the gangway and went in to gather his belongings. He only had a handful more possessions than when he had left Tararia, but it didn't feel right to leave it all behind. He sighed. He had to tell

Thom he was leaving.

Cris found Thom in the flight deck, reviewing the ship's inventory. "Thom?"

The captain looked up. "What is it?"

"Thom, something's come up." Cris swallowed, a sudden heaviness in his chest. "I've just been offered a training opportunity with the TSS."

Thom searched Cris' face. "Are you accepting?"

Cris nodded. "This is something I have to do."

The captain sighed and stood up. "When?"

"Right now. I'm sorry."

Thom nodded, processing the loss of his travel companion. "I understand." He took Cris' hand, shook it. "I always suspected you were destined for greater things. I hope you find what you're looking for."

Cris looked down. *He might not know my real name, but he always saw me for who I am.* "Thank you for everything. I couldn't have asked for more."

The captain smiled and patted Cris on the shoulder. "Best of luck, Cris."

"Thank you, Thom. You too." Cris turned to go.

"Oh, and here." Thom grabbed his Fastara deck. "Take these."

Cris smiled. "I'll teach everyone who'll listen."

Before he could change his mind, Cris exited the flight deck and hurried down the gangway to meet the waiting Agents. With only his single bag slung over his shoulder, Cris felt bare and alone.

Jarek and Dodes led Cris away from the *Exler* toward their TSS transport ship. The Agents were unlike anyone he had met before. They moved with a sort of elegance, as though they were one with their surroundings. Even their tailored black uniforms, which were casual compared to attire of the Tararian Guard, projected a sense of regality, making Cris feel like he would be underdressed even while wearing his finest suit. There was also an energy about them that he couldn't quite identify—a magnetism that made him have difficulty looking away.

Over the last year, Cris had become used to blending in and downplaying the authority that had been ingrained in him through years of tutoring. Now, even in the most refined state he could muster, he still felt insignificant compared to the Agents. *How long before the TSS changes me, too?*

As they passed through the spaceport, passersby looked on with wonder and gave the party a wide berth. On the rare occasions Cris had been permitted to visit Sieten, he had received similar looks from the city's residents. *There's a sense of awe, but in the same way someone admires a majestic animal that could readily kill its handlers. What will that make me, as both an Agent and dynastic leader?*

Cris' thoughts were interrupted by a glimpse of the TSS ship in the distance down the spaceport's corridor. He had previously seen TSS vessels while visiting a Sietinen shipyard—one of the ancillary businesses to SiNavTech. The TSS vessel stood out from the other crafts in the port by its iridescent hull and smooth lines. The materials for the hull were far too expensive for everyday civilian use, but the superior impact absorption was an asset for combat applications and for minimizing the structural stress of subspace travel. At eighty meters long, this particular craft was much smaller than those he had previously seen, though it made sense that the Agents wouldn't take a warship on a recruitment mission.

"How long will it take to get to Headquarters?" Cris asked as they approached the ship.

"About four hours," Jarek replied.

"I didn't realize it was located so close to the outer colonies," Cris commented.

"It's not," Jarek replied. "Headquarters is located in Earth's moon."

"Earth?" Cris asked, incredulous. "That seems like a strange place for TSS Headquarters."

"What makes you say that?" Dodes asked.

"Earth isn't part of the Taran government, for one."

"Which makes it a perfect location for training those with telekinetic abilities, doesn't it?" Jarek pointed out.

"I guess it does." *Far from the control of the Priesthood.* Like most children, Cris had learned the story of Earth as a cautionary tale. Over millennia, Taran descendants seeking to escape the perceived oppression of Tararian rule had fled to Earth and mingled with the native population born from ancient panspermia. Each group of Taran colonists had brought with them elements of the unique cultures from their home worlds, but they shared the common vision of a new start—leaving behind the advanced technologies that connected them to the rest of Tarans in an attempt to disappear. As the "lost colony" of Earth gave rise and fall to its own great civilizations, Tarans had watched their divergent brethren from a distance—but apparently from far closer than most of Earth's population would have ever imagined. *Perhaps the location is also an homage to our lost relationship.*

"Headquarters is within a subspace containment shell inside the moon. Our space dock is fixed just above the surface on the dark side, so we keep to ourselves," Jarek continued.

Cris' brow furrowed. "Subspace containment shell?"

Jarek smiled. "A sustained subspace pocket surrounded by a really big wall. Basically, breaking into Headquarters would be extremely difficult."

"I'll take your word for it," Cris replied. *I guess if their ships are any indication, the rest of their tech is pretty advanced, too.*

"It all might seem strange to you now, but we like being a little hidden," Jarek said as he led the way up the gangway to the ship.

It is pretty out of the way... "Wait, you said it would only take four hours to get there. Isn't Earth in a sector that's two or three weeks' travel from here?"

Dodes smirked. "With a civilian jump drive, maybe."

Is there another kind? "What does the TSS use?"

"We have a long-range subspace transit," Jarek explained. "It works the same basic way as commercial vessels—locking onto SiNavTech beacons. But, rather than the short jumps used by cargo freighters and civilian transports, our ships can lock onto beacons at much farther intervals to expedite the jump. Since our drives don't require cool-down, travel time is reduced by a factor of thirty."

That puts the entire galaxy within easy reach. "I've heard theories about long-duration drives, but I didn't know the technology was ever developed."

Jarek nodded. "There are many ways the TSS is outside the mainstream. Travel technology is one of the big ones."

They reached the top of the gangway. Inside, the TSS ship was simply appointed but comfortable. Gray carpet covered the floor of the hall, and metal wall panels were inset with tan accents. Jarek headed down the hall to the right.

The technology divide is so much bigger than I ever imagined. "I'm surprised I never heard about the extent of SiNavTech's work with the TSS."

"I'm sure you would have eventually," Jarek said. "But it is kept pretty need-to-know."

What else haven't I been told? "I guess so."

The hall ended at a lounge room. In the center of the space, there were four plush chairs upholstered in a matte black fabric, which circled a low table with chrome legs and a glass top. An expansive window filled the outer wall, and one of the side walls had a broad viewscreen.

"I hope this will be acceptable for the next few hours," Jarek said.

It beats the flight deck on the Exler. "It'll be fine, thank you."

"Make yourself comfortable," Jarek said and gestured toward the chairs.

Cris set his travel bag down on the floor next to one of the chairs with a good view out the window. He settled into the chair, and Dodes took a seat across from him.

Jarek remained by the door. "Excuse me, I'll get us underway." He inclined his head to Cris and left the cabin.

Dodes pulled a handheld out from his pocket and began looking at something on the device.

Cris took the opportunity to clear his head. He closed his eyes. *I never thought I would be joining the TSS. Especially not like this. I always thought growing my abilities would be useful and fun, but now I'm scared to see what I'll be able to do. I never wanted to hurt anyone.*

After a few minutes, Cris felt the low rumble of the jump drive through the floor. Unlike the *Exler*, the vibration seemed muted and controlled. He opened his eyes. The stars out the window slowly became masked by blue-green light as the ship slipped into subspace.

"It's nice to just be a passenger for a change," Cris said.

"I'll bet," Dodes replied, looking up from his handheld. "Relax while you can. The TSS isn't exactly known for easing people in gently."

"What should I expect?"

"I honestly don't know. You're a unique case. The High Commander wants to meet you, and he'll figure out where to place you."

Cris crossed his arms, pulling inward. "Is it because of what I did earlier?" *Do they also think I'm dangerous?*

Dodes hesitated. "Yes, but not just that. You have a lot more potential than most."

Cris looked down. "I didn't know I could do those things."

"Soon enough you'll be able to do a lot more."

Cris leaned back in his chair and stared out the window at

the swirling blue-green sea of light. *I hope this is the right choice.*

"Did you really have another option?" Dodes asked in response to Cris' thought.

Cris realized he had let his mental guard lapse and raised it again. "No, not anymore." *Not now that I know what I can do.*

"We'll take care of you, don't worry," Dodes said.

At least I'll finally be around other people like me. Cris stared back out the window. *Maybe I'll finally fit in.*

<> <> <>

"Sir, we have him. It sounds like he wants to join."

Banks leaped up from his desk and walked toward the main viewscreen to speak with Jarek. *Thank the stars, finally!* "Good. Did you have any trouble?"

"Yes, actually. Much more than expected," Jarek said.

"Did he resist?"

Jarek's brow furrowed. "No, he came quite easily."

"Then how so?"

"He was attacked."

No, don't tell me... "Attacked? By whom?"

"An assassin from the Priesthood. They must have been acting on the same information about his whereabouts that we were."

Bomax! What were they thinking? Banks was careful to hide his indignation. "How did he escape?"

Jarek looked away. "Sir, he 'stopped time'."

Banks tensed. "What?" *How is that possible? I know he's gifted, but that...*

"I don't know, sir. He seemed distraught. I asked him afterward, and he said he'd never done it before."

If he really did... "It's unheard of, pulling off that maneuver without extensive coaching."

Jarek looked shaken. "I know, sir. I barely knew what I was seeing. I've only witnessed it once before. But that's not all."

Banks took a slow breath. "There's more?"

"Then he threw the assassin against the wall telekinetically. I was struck by the power of it—absolutely astounding. There was a great measure of control, even though he claimed to not know what he was doing."

"This development complicates matters considerably." *I can't possibly put him in with other new Trainees. Not with that level of ability.* "But he's safe?"

"Yes, sir. Shaken, but unharmed."

Banks nodded. "Good. We'll decide what to do after I meet with him." *After all of our careful planning, we're back to making up a strategy as we go.*

"Yes, sir." Jarek inclined his head.

"Dismissed."

◄ CHAPTER 7 ►

The TSS ship dropped out of subspace. In the distance, Cris glimpsed Earth with its large continents that in some ways reminded him of Tararia. The planet was soon obscured by the moon that stood out as a white orb against the surrounding darkness, barren compared to most of the moons he had encountered in his travels.

The TSS ship taxied toward a sprawling space dock fixed with a gravity anchor fifteen kilometers out from the hemisphere of the moon facing away from Earth. There were crafts of all sizes, from shuttles only four meters in length to massive warships. Cris exhaled slowly with wonder. *I haven't seen a fleet like that outside of a shipyard.*

"It's something, isn't it?" Dodes commented. "And to think most people on Earth have no idea all this is up here."

Cris couldn't take his eyes off the window. "It's impressive, for sure."

The door opened, and Jarek looked in. "Time to get going."

"Come on," Dodes said, gesturing toward the door.

Cris tore himself away and grabbed his bag off the floor. A wave of nerves suddenly struck him. Joining the TSS would set a new future for him. A path he never thought was possible. *But I need to do this. It's the only way I'll ever learn to use my abilities.* He swallowed and took a deep breath. Resolute, he followed Dodes into the hall.

Jarek led the way to the gangway off of the ship. The gangway was glass on either side, with a metal floor and a thin strip of metal along the top. The transparent walls afforded an impressive view of the moon's cratered surface and the surrounding ships in the port. The lights along the port's structure reflected off of the iridescent hulls of the ships, making the more distant vessels look like gems against the dark starscape beyond.

At the bottom of the gangway, Jarek turned to Cris. "Best wishes. I know the TSS will be quite a change for you, but I hope you'll find a sense of community here."

"Thank you. I hope so, too." Cris shifted the pack on his shoulder. *For the first time, I'll be around other people like me.*

Jarek and Dodes took Cris down one of the wings of the spaceport. The port was unadorned, with plain grated metal floors and matte metal structural beams. Curved glass panels swept toward the ceiling.

They approached a row of small shuttles. Waiting for them was a woman dressed in dark gray. She appeared to be in her early-thirties, with dark eyes and hair pulled back into a tight bun.

"This is where we leave you," Jarek said. "Trisa is one of our Militia officers. She'll take you to the High Commander."

"Okay. Well, I'll see you around," Cris said.

"Yes, I'm sure," Jarek replied.

"Take care," added Dodes.

Trisa held out her arm toward one of the waiting shuttles. "This way, please."

The oblong shuttle was only four meters long. Windows wrapped around the perimeter, making it difficult to distinguish between the front and back of the craft. A door on the side connected directly to the spaceport's corridor. The interior was one open room with dark gray padded seats along the walls, each with a four-point harness. Cris took a seat in the middle, and noticed a control panel inlaid in the wall next to the door.

Trisa sat down next to the control panel. She didn't secure herself in a harness, so Cris left his off, as well. Without a word, Trisa made a few inputs on the panel. The shuttle door closed with a hiss and the craft pulled away from the port. It glided toward the surface of the moon, accelerating.

Cris swiveled around to stare out the window at the cratered, dusty surface. *Is there really a whole facility inside there?* It looked desolate and barren, but an illuminated ship port stood out at the base of one of the craters. The port was a simple structure consisting of three corridors with docking slots for transport shuttles to either side along each of the wings. Approximately half of the slots were occupied by a craft.

The shuttle slowed as it approached an open docking slot between several other shuttles. It set down with a barely perceptible bump. The door automatically sealed with a portal in the wall of the corridor, and the door slid open after a moment.

Cris gulped. *I guess I'm committed now.*

Trisa led Cris across the port through a security checkpoint at the end of the corridor. Beyond the security gate, the port opened up into a central dome at the intersection of the three branches. On the far side, there was a bank of what looked to be elevator doors arranged in a half-circle.

Trisa stopped in front of the doors. After a minute, one of the doors opened, revealing an elevator car with an upholstered seat around the perimeter and room for a dozen people.

Cris took a seat along the back wall, and Trisa sat near the door. As soon as the door closed, there was an initial feeling of acceleration. Trisa glanced over at Cris on occasion, but made no effort to converse. Minutes of silence passed. The only indication of movement was a pulsing white light to either side of the door. Suddenly, there was a loud thud outside.

Cris' pulse spiked, startled after the quiet. "What was that?"

"Entering the containment lock for the subspace shell around Headquarters," Trisa stated. She folded her arms and leaned back.

She said that like it's a normal thing. Cris leaned back on the seat and tried to relax.

Eventually, the elevator slowed and came to a rest. Cris' heart-rate quickened as the doors opened, revealing a circular lobby surrounded by elevator doors. The floor was dark gray marble with decorative black inlay. *This is way fancier than I pictured.* Trisa headed straight across the lobby, entering a surprisingly decorated hallway. Cris looked around in wonder at the carpeted floor and wood paneling, with show weapons and holopaintings lining the walls. They went past several offices before the hall ended in a set of double wooden doors.

"Here is the office of the TSS High Commander," Trisa said. "This is his jurisdiction and you are his subordinate."

"Understood."

"All right. Go in," she said.

Cris nodded. Trisa swung one of the doors inward, and she directed Cris into the High Commander's office.

Cris' first impression of the room was that it was too ornate, like the hallway, to serve much practical purpose. He had been brought up with the utmost luxuries, but he had always been under the impression that the TSS would have no use for elaborate furnishings. He did have to admit there was good taste behind the selection of the leather couch and carved wooden desk, but it all seemed superfluous until he examined the items more closely. The couch was facing an extensive viewscreen integrated into the side wall. The desk was decorative, but its touch-surface top also served as a workstation. The display cases likely held the High Commander's personal combat implements, rather than purely show weapons, as Cris had initially thought. Once he looked at it that way, Cris realized the TSS simply had style.

The High Commander stood on the far side of the room across from the door, seemingly staring out at the snow-capped mountains depicted in a holopainting on the wall. The moment the door closed, he turned to look at Cris. He wasn't presently wearing the tinted glasses typically worn by Agents, so Cris could clearly see the peculiar eyes associated with advanced telekinetic abilities. The eyes were the High Commander's natural gray color, but they seemed to be slightly bioluminescent—glowing with a captivating inner light.

The High Commander stepped forward and stopped in front of Cris. "I'm High Commander Jason Banks," he said with a voice of obvious authority. "You're Cristoph Sietinen, I presume."

Cris nodded. "Yes, sir, I am. I go by 'Cris' most of the time, though." He looked the High Commander over. He had dark hair and appeared to only be around thirty-years-old, though that seemed improbable given his rank. *He carries himself as if he were much older. He must be at least a decade older than he appears.*

"Well, Cris, you're a difficult person to find." Banks looked at him levelly.

Resisting the urge to squirm under the High Commander's scrutinizing gaze, Cris ventured a smile. "Then I accomplished my aim. Until you found me."

"You were careless. It almost got you killed."

He's not messing around. "In retrospect, I would have done things differently, that's for sure."

Banks sighed. "That's all you have to say for yourself?"

Cris faltered. *What does he want me to say?* "I'm sorry."

"Don't say things you don't mean. It's unbecoming."

Stars! Maybe aligning with the TSS was a mistake. "Then what do you want? *You* brought *me* here. I was perfectly happy on the *Exler*, minding my own business—"

"Hardly!" Banks' glared at Cris, stern. "Do you realize what would happen if the general population heard the Sietinen heir was threatening the Priesthood?"

He knows about that? "How can you defend the Priesthood? They hate people like us." Cris felt his face flush. "I thought the TSS of all organizations would see things my way."

Banks laughed. "Your way? You have so much to learn."

Cris was taken aback. "Maybe I should just go."

"Go ahead. It wouldn't surprise me."

What's his problem? Cris glanced toward the door but stood his ground. "You went to an awful lot of trouble to find me, only to let me walk away."

"I'd rather you walk away now than when you have a ship full of people counting on you," the High Commander replied.

Cris crossed his arms. "I wouldn't abandon my crew."

"You ran away from Tararia," Banks shot back. "Why should I expect you to be any more loyal to the TSS?"

I'm not disloyal to Tararia. I'd just rather be here. "I want to learn about my abilities."

Banks looked skeptical. "And once you've mastered them? Given your track record, I would expect you to walk away whenever something new and interesting caught your eye."

"That's not why I left."

"Well, I have no idea what will make you stay here." The High Commander shrugged. "Jarek and Dodes brought you in because that was their last standing order, but after the way you've behaved, I don't know if I want you to be part of the TSS."

Stars! Is he serious? "So you'd turn me loose, knowing the Priesthood will kill me the first chance they get?"

Banks' eyes narrowed. "I'm simply not convinced you're cut out to be an Agent. The TSS isn't a good fit for people who like to take the easy route."

Cris stared back at the High Commander with disbelief. "You think it was easy for me to leave Tararia? I didn't want to go. I just knew if I didn't, I'd be stifled for life."

"The TSS won't exactly give you freedom, either," Banks stated. "We can teach you how to use your abilities, but it's a lifetime commitment of service in return. I don't think you're ready for that."

"I was born into a lifetime of service." *That responsibility isn't new to me.*

Banks tilted his head. "But you ran away."

"I didn't run away!" Cris insisted. *I left, but I didn't forget my responsibility. I'll be there when it matters.*

Banks stepped toward Cris. "Take some personal responsibility! You'll make a piss-poor leader if you always blame others for everything that doesn't go 'your way'. So do you want to keep running, or do you want to man up and do something that really matters?"

It took all of Cris' will to keep from cowering as the High Commander approached. *I was only trying to be true to myself.* "All I've ever wanted is to find a real home."

The High Commander softened. "We can give you that, Cris. But I need to know that you're fully vested. You have so much potential—we can unlock abilities that you never dreamed possible. But I can't let you gain all that power and then go rogue."

Cris straightened. "I only left so that I could become the kind of leader Tararia deserves."

"You've gone about it pretty poorly," Banks said.

Cris looked him in the eye. "Then show me another way." *I need the TSS now. I don't have anywhere else to go.*

"So you do want to be here?" Banks asked.

"Yes. Please, just give me a chance."

Banks let out a slow breath. "Even if I do let you join, I don't know where we'd place you."

Cris looked down. "Find a place. I *need* to be here. And not just because it's away from the Priesthood—this is the only place where I can learn to become my full self." *Besides, no one has ever put me in my place like he did, especially knowing who I am. That's the kind of push that will help me grow.*

Banks was silent, pensive. He cocked his head slightly as he looked Cris over from head to foot. "You demonstrated you already know how to handle yourself, as far as hand-to-hand combat is concerned. What about telepathy?"

Does that mean I'm in? "I received some basic lessons from a Court Advisor, but I haven't practiced much since I left the family compound. With things as they are on Tararia, I was never able to practice anything too advanced."

Banks nodded. "That's what makes things so tricky. You already know more than any other incoming Trainee. Yet, even if we enrolled you directly as an Initiate, you don't have the requisite experience in free-fall spatial awareness training."

Cris hung his head, growing increasingly more concerned about his prospects with the TSS. "No, I don't." *What would I do if he turns me away? Would I even be safe at the Sietinen estate?*

"One of the few options available," Banks continued, "would be to put you into an apprenticeship with an Agent for a few months to catch you up to a second or third year Initiate class. Would you be comfortable with that arrangement?"

I've lived my whole life with private tutors—why would I be uncomfortable? "That would be fine. Whatever you think is best." *Just please let me stay.*

Banks evaluated Cris, seeming to weigh something that was unseen. "Very well."

Cris perked up. "Does that mean I can join?"

The High Commander nodded. "Yes. I just wanted to make sure you were here for the right reasons."

"I like to think I am."

Banks smiled. "I can see that. Now, I don't suppose you have a preference for an area of specialization?"

Cris shook his head. "No. I'm sorry, but I am not familiar

with the different classes of Agents. One of the few TSS-trained people I know is my former combat instructor from the Tararian Guard, but he was Militia."

"I see," the High Commander said. "Well, since you certainly won't be in Militia, I suppose you could be placed along the Command track with an Agent in Primus, our top class. With your background, you're a natural fit for a leadership role, so a support position in the Sacon or Trion Agent class doesn't make sense. Though we select only a small number of trainees with the highest potential for Primus—especially the Command track—I'm not too concerned about you meeting the requirements of the designation. If you apply yourself, I'm sure you could graduate as one of the best in your cohort. You have too much potential to fail completely."

"Sir, what is this 'potential' that keeps being brought up? Does it have something to do with what I did at the spaceport?"

Banks paused for a moment. "Everyone has an innate level of telepathic and telekinetic ability, which varies greatly among individuals. Those abilities manifest in different ways. From what I heard, you created a spatial disruption at the spaceport. We often call it 'stopping time', but it's actually telekinetic dislocation—you hovered on the edge of subspace, where the perception of time passage is different. Very few can do it."

"So why me?"

"Luck of the genetic draw," the High Commander replied with a slight smile. "It is a sign of potential in other areas, too. You can go far."

"Lucky me, then," Cris said. *Is that really it?* "I'll try my best to live up to your expectations."

Banks nodded. "Just apply yourself."

I'll do what it takes to succeed, but what does the TSS want in return? "There is another question, sir."

"Yes?"

"A few weeks ago, I had an encounter with a merchant. He

spoke of a war in the outer territories. He said that the TSS told their trainees the truth about what's going on at the end of their first year."

Banks swallowed, barely perceptible. "You can't believe everything you hear at spaceports."

"But, *is* there a war?" Cris pressed.

The High Commander took a deep breath. "There is mounting tension with a race called the Bakzen. We suspect it will escalate to full-out war within our lifetime. Since the TSS is a lifetime commitment, we need individuals who will be steadfast to the cause when the time comes. So, we give our trainees the chance to leave after their first year if they are not willing to participate in a war, should they ever be called upon." He looked Cris in the eye. "Does that change your decision to train with the TSS?"

Cris looked inward. *I have to stay, regardless of what may be going on elsewhere in the galaxy. The TSS can give me what I need.* "No, sir. I would gladly fight with the TSS."

Banks nodded. "That's good to hear." He paused. "You know," he began, "I'm sure your parents would like to know that you're safe and that they can halt their detectives. Since you're seventeen now, once you sign the training contract, we can grant you immunity so they can't bring you home against your will."

Thank the stars! My parents would never consent to this. "Yes, I'll let them know. Thank you."

"I can draw up the contract now before you contact them," Banks offered. He took a step toward his desk.

"That would be great. One more thing though…"

Banks stopped. "Hmm?"

"I would like to keep my true identity confidential. As you know, sir, the Sietinen family name comes with a reputation." *The last thing I want is to go back to that way of life.* He couldn't pass up the chance to truly begin anew, and in a far better way than on the *Exler*. He could become a worthy leader—prepared to face the changes on Tararia in the future.

"As you wish," Banks agreed. "The contract must be with your legal name, but you may go publicly by something else if you like. Others do the same thing. Do you already have a name in mind?"

Cris smiled. "I went by 'Cris Sights' on the cargo freighter." *This is it! I actually got away for good.*

High Commander Banks nodded. "Well, Cris Sights, welcome to the Tararian Selective Service."

<> <> <>

Banks sat down on the couch in the middle of his office, unsure how to proceed. Cris Sights, as he was to be known, was perhaps the most gifted student the TSS had ever seen. He was confident and insightful, but also quick to anger—though that will mellow with time and the discipline of training. Banks sensed the power in him that Jarek had witnessed; was cautious of it. Cris was not someone to deceive, but that was precisely what had to be done.

The High Commander sat for a long while, pondering the situation. *The Priesthood tried to kill him. Why? We can't afford to start all over again. They can't be foolish enough to think we could hold on that much longer... But why did they want him eliminated?*

"CACI," Banks intoned, directing his attention to the Central Artificial Computer Intelligence interface for the TSS Mainframe via the viewscreen on the wall, "contact the Priesthood. Let them know I want to talk to them immediately about Cristoph Sietinen."

As expected, it did not take long for the call to be accepted. The life-like image of a figure robed in black appeared on the screen, piercing red-brown eyes shone out through the shadow cast by the hood. Banks stood to address the High Priest.

"Thank you for granting me audience," he said in Old Taran, the standard language of the Priesthood. The words felt strange compared to the galactic common New Taran.

"I was told you wanted to discuss Cristoph Sietinen."

"Yes," Banks replied. "We agreed that this was a TSS matter. Sending an assassin—"

The Priest gave a slight nod. "If we had been able to properly evaluate him a year before, as we wanted, it would not have come to that."

What was there to evaluate? We already knew everything we needed to. "What is the problem with him, exactly? I thought he had all the qualities we hoped for."

"He is too independent. Powerful, yes, but he will not easily be bent to our wills. Escaping from Tararia was proof enough, but he's also publicly spoken out against the Priesthood."

That's what makes him perfect. We need someone with initiative. "It's the child he will one day father that matters. In the meantime, the TSS can mold him. He is eager to learn."

"For the sake of the entire Taran race, I hope you are right."

"Your dissatisfaction with his brother set us back twenty years, as it was. You waited far too long to decide what to do with him." *If only he had come to the TSS when we first extended an offer.*

"We are aware. But he refused to embrace his abilities. We had no other choice."

And so he met his end in a "tragic accident." "The anti-telekinesis sentiment is dangerous. I've warned you—"

"You know the reasons why it's necessary."

"It's crippled us—"

"Perhaps in a few more years we can reconsider." The Priest's level gaze was one of finality.

Banks looked down and took a deep breath to calm himself. "All concerns about Cris aside, we need to move forward with him. He's in our custody now, and I'd appreciate you consulting me first if you have any reservations in the future."

The Priest reluctantly inclined his head. "What does he know of our intentions?"

"Very little. I'm sure he'll figure out that we're keeping something from him, but there's no cause for concern. As for the Bakzen, he will learn the standard story."

"Good. You have your mandate." The Priest ended the transmission.

‹   CHAPTER 8   ›

Cris quickly learned that life with the TSS was far more
exhausting than he could have ever imagined.

Immediately upon leaving the High Commander's office, he
was ushered back into the central elevator and taken further
into the Headquarters facility. Without warning, he was run
through a barrage of tests. Hours passed as he took written
exams, was placed in all manner of scanners and was hooked up
to more machines than he could count. Tired and cranky, he
was beginning to regret his decision to join the TSS when
suddenly it was over. An attendant handed him a set of light
blue clothes and he was left alone in a small room to change.

Cris donned the pants, t-shirt, and jacket, then collapsed on
the single, low bench in the room. He had no idea how much
time had gone by, but it felt like days. *What was I thinking
coming here?*

He closed his eyes and was on the verge of dozing off when
the door opened. A man in all black with tinted glasses stood in
the doorway. He was tall and had dark features, and he carried
himself with assurance. An Agent. Cris blinked wearily.

The Agent cracked a smile. "Looks like they wore you out."
He removed his tinted glasses, revealing luminescent warm
brown eyes.

Cris let out a non-committal groan.

"I'm Agent Poltar. I've been assigned to train you over the

next few months."

Cris tried to rally, but couldn't quite muster the energy. "Pleasure to meet you, sir. I'm excited to get started."

The Agent smiled. "I'll be nice and let you rest up before we dive into things. Let me show you to your quarters."

Poltar led Cris to the second level of the Headquarters structure, making small-talk along the way. Cris learned that Poltar was from the eastern part of the First Region on Tararia and had been with the TSS since he was sixteen-years-old. Cris shared a little of his time on the *Exler*.

When they exited the elevator, Poltar said, "We were unsure where to house you since you're in between ranks right now. At first, we were going to put you in Agent's quarters temporarily, but then we thought it best that you be around fellow trainees. In the end, we decided to place you in Junior Agent quarters for the time being."

They walked down a long hallway with carpeting and paneling similar to the top level by the High Commander's office, though not as ornate. Small fern-like plants with delicate oval leaves were placed every few meters, contained in glass cylinders with down-lights. Holopaintings of nebulae lined the walls.

Poltar stopped at a door halfway down the hall, marked as JAP-227. "Fortunately, we had an opening with some of our top Junior Agent trainees. They'll take good care of you." Poltar pressed the buzzer by the door.

A young man with light brown hair and hazel eyes slid open the door; he looked to be a few years older than Cris. He wore dark blue clothes, which Cris had gathered were for Junior Agents. "Good evening, Agent Poltar."

"Hi, Scott. This is Cris Sights. He's the new recruit who'll be staying with you for a while."

"Right!" Scott extended his hand to Cris for a handshake. "Scott Wincowski, nice to meet you."

Cris grasped his hand awkwardly, not used to the colloquial greeting. "You too, thanks for having me."

"Sure thing." Scott stood aside to give Cris room to come in. "I can take it from here tonight, Agent Poltar."

"Thank you. Cris, I'll be by at 08:00 to begin your training tomorrow. Rest up."

"Will do. Good night. And thank you, sir."

Poltar nodded and left in the direction of the elevators.

"Come in," Scott said, gesturing to Cris. Cris took his lead.

The door opened into the common room of the quarters. Like the hallway, the living room presented like a well-appointed home. Padded carpet covered the floor, a plush sectional couch faced a large viewscreen on the wall and holoart depicting exotic mountain ranges and beaches lined the copper-colored walls. A table surrounded by four chairs stood at the back of the room.

"You're quite lucky, you know," Scott said as Cris entered. "I had to sleep on a tiny bunk in a room with four other guys for the first year I was here."

"I would have been happy with anything, just to be here." Cris took in the room. It was spacious and inviting after his sterile cabin on the *Exler*.

"Regardless, they must see something special in you."

"I'll try my hardest." *I may even surprise myself.*

"Well, anyway," Scott moved backward past the couch, "let me show you your bedroom." Cris noticed two doorways on each side of the common room. Scott approached the doorway in the back right. "We're still down a roommate, even with you here," Scott went on. "They like to pair Junior Agents in multiple cohorts so there are mentorship opportunities. We just had the two oldest roommates graduate."

"I take it most Junior Agents don't get brand new Trainees for roommates," Cris ventured.

Scott studied Cris, serious. "No, never."

Cris dropped his eyes to the floor, feeling out of place.

"As I said, they must see something in you." Scott slid the door to the bedchamber open. It took Cris a moment to realize that he hadn't physically touched the door. "This will be your room."

Careful not to gape at Scott's open use of telekinesis, Cris peeked inside. The room was compact but not cramped. It was simply furnished, containing a large bed, corner desk and dresser. The bag containing his personal articles from the *Exler* was placed on the bed. "Excellent." *This is a resort compared to where I've been for the last year.* The bed beckoned to him.

"The bathroom is through there." Scott gestured to a wider doorway at the back of the common room. "They set up a locker in there for you."

"Where do you eat?" Now that he was standing still, Cris felt hunger mounting.

"They didn't feed you?" Scott seemed a little irritated, but not at Cris directly.

Cris shook his head. "I've been on the move constantly since I got here. I don't even know how long it's been."

Scott looked Cris over again. "You'll never live it down if I take you to the mess hall like this, looking wiped out and lost. Not a great first impression. Do you think a couple protein bars would hold you over until the morning?"

Cris shrugged. "I'll take whatever I can get."

"Let's see…" Scott rummaged through a cabinet by the table and chairs at the back of the common room. He produced two bars in shiny metallic wrappers. "These should take the edge off, at least."

"Thanks." Cris took the bars from Scott. "I have no idea how anything works around here." *And I thought that the* Exler *was different than Tararia. This is something else entirely.*

"Sure." Scott hesitated. "My room's the one right across the way if you need anything else."

"Thank you. See you in the morning." Cris entered his room and closed the door.

The lights faded on automatically as he entered and a screen on the wall behind the desk illuminated as soon as the door was closed, displaying the TSS logo. Cris ripped open one of the protein bars and devoured it. He kicked off his shoes and was about to sit down on the bed when he noticed that the desktop was a large touchscreen, similar to his desk back home. There were also a handheld and a tablet sitting on the desktop to charge. Still chewing, he placed his palm on the desktop.

"Welcome, Cris Sights," said a friendly female voice. "Would you like to configure your preferences?" The TSS logo on the screen changed to read: "Welcome." The sleek black desktop surface illuminated, and various colored menus and windows appeared. Cris was especially taken by the icon for the TSS Mainframe.

Cris sighed, noting the late hour on the computer clock. "Not right now," he replied, though a large part of him wanted to explore. "Can you set an alarm for the morning?"

"Yes. Please state the desired time for the alarm."

Cris did some quick mental math. "07:15."

"Alarm set."

Cris grabbed the handheld from the desk. Thin and the size of his palm, it appeared to be solid, but he tugged the edges and the device slid open, displaying a screen on one side with an opaque backside for privacy. He swiped along the screen, activating a holographic projection of the contents on the screen, which he could manipulate in the air. He closed the device, and browsed the settings for the external notifications that illuminated in the otherwise smooth black outer casing. It was just like the handheld he'd used back home. *VComm has a presence even within the TSS. I guess I shouldn't be surprised, given they use SiNavTech beacons for navigation.* He set the handheld back on the desk.

A yawn overpowered Cris. He shoved his travel bag onto the ground. After stripping down to his underwear, he climbed in bed, feeling his muscles relax as he eased into the soft mattress. "Lights off," he ordered, already drifting to sleep.

<>

Soft beeping intruded on Cris' dream, getting louder. He opened his eyes.

The screen on the wall displayed the time, 07:15. Cris rubbed his eyes and stretched.

He dressed and wandered into the living room. Scott and another young man were stretched out on the sectional couch, apparently reading on their tablets. They glanced up when Cris emerged.

"Good morning," Scott said. "How'd you sleep?"

"Really well."

"So, Cris, this is Jon Lambren. His room is the one next to mine."

Jon gave a little wave but barely lifted his eyes from whatever he was reading. His dark hair was cut short and he had a seriousness about him.

"Hi," Cris said as though he hadn't noticed Jon's disinterest.

Scott's attention returned to his own tablet. Cris let them be and headed into the bathroom. He was pleased to see that the facilities were smartly designed to easily accommodate four people. He found all the necessities in a locker with his name on it, including a change of clothes. After the nonstop events of the previous day, he was happy to take a leisurely pace getting ready.

Cris emerged from the bathroom feeling ready to tackle whatever Agent Poltar could throw at him. Since he still had some time before Poltar was scheduled to arrive, Cris decided to take the opportunity to do some of the electronic sleuthing he had been too tired to attempt the night before.

CACI—which he learned was the interactive interface for the TSS Mainframe—walked him through the configuration of his personal notifications, gesture calibration and setup of his telecommunication accounts. As he walked through the setup, he munched on the second protein bar Scott had given him the night before, pleasantly surprised by how filling it was. He was just finishing when a window popped up with a video feed, showing Poltar standing at the front door.

"Meet me out here, Cris," Poltar said, looking straight into the camera. The exploration of the TSS network would have to wait.

Cris grabbed a light blue jacket to match the rest of his uniform and hurried out. Scott and Jon were already gone.

"Good morning, sir. I can't wait to get started." Cris closed the door to his quarters.

"We'll see how long you can hold onto that enthusiasm."

Poltar took Cris down the long central elevator to the bottom level of the Headquarters structure once again. This time, Cris noticed that the elevator passed through another containment lock like the one coming from the moon's surface.

Cris was wary. The last time he was down there, it had meant seemingly endless testing. *Is this a place of torture?*

Poltar led Cris down a hall that bore no resemblance to the elegant comfort of the upper levels. Though the floor was still carpeted, it was a plain industrial gray, and the walls were unadorned metal that looked to have had little treatment after fabrication. Cris followed Poltar through the halls in silence, trying to decide if he'd rather know what he was in for or remain sheltered by ignorance for as long as possible. They passed no one in the corridor.

Poltar stopped in front of a nondescript door identical to a dozen others they had already passed. The doors were placed far apart, each one was smooth metal recessed in the wall, with glowing red or blue lights illuminating the perimeter. A control panel was positioned next to each. Poltar made some inputs on the panel by the selected door, and the light turned from blue to red.

"Let's see what you can do." Poltar grinned at Cris.

Cris swallowed.

The door opened, revealing a plain room. The threshold between the hallway and the adjoining wall of the room was nearly a meter. What appeared to be a door was centered on the back wall, a square too high off the ground to step through. The surface of the room was completely smooth, aside from handholds recessed around the door on the far side. Poltar stepped inside.

Cris hesitated. "What is this?"

"Have you ever been in freefall before?"

Freefall! His stomach tightened with the memory of his first night on the *Exler*. "Once."

"So what are you waiting for?"

Cris stepped into the room. "Sorry, sir."

Poltar activated a control panel inside the room, and the outer door closed. He placed his tinted glasses into a sealed pocket inside his jacket, then moved to the back wall and grabbed a handhold. Cris followed his lead. "Take slow, steady breaths," Poltar said. "It can be unsettling at first."

The energy in the air around Cris changed. His stomach dropped, and then began rising into his mouth. He felt like he was being stretched and compressed at the same time. Ever so gradually, he felt himself rising off the ground. He tried to keep his feet rooted on the floor, but the struggle made him queasy so he relaxed. He floated upward until he was parallel with the door. Concentrating on his breathing, he centered his mind and tried to settle the queasiness in his stomach.

"Are you doing all right?" Poltar asked, looking Cris over.

Cris nodded to test himself. *Much better this time.* "A little unsteady, but I think I'm okay." *I'd die of embarrassment if I threw up in front of an Agent.*

"Good." Poltar looked pleased.

The square door in the center of the back wall opened automatically. Cris peered into the next room with wonder. The entire room was black, illuminated only by pinpricks of light that looked like stars across all the surfaces. There was no sense of up or down, and Cris had difficulty judging the size of the space.

"This is one of our spatial awareness training chambers," Poltar explained. "We'll also work on your telekinetic skills, once we've covered some of the basics. This setting is ideal for honing your sense of what's around you and learning how to manipulate your environment."

Cris took an unsteady breath. "Tell me what to do."

Poltar pushed himself into the chamber. It was eerie to watch him glide without his overcoat fluttering. He moved deftly, a master of his surroundings. He stretched out a hand and stopped himself in the middle of open space.

Cris stared at him in wonder. *How did he do that?*

"Come here," Poltar commanded.

Cris let go of the handhold and pushed off the door frame with his feet. As soon as he was out of contact with the wall, he realized he had pushed far too hard. His aim was true in the direction of Poltar. Too true. He panicked, seeing he was on a collision course with his teacher. Poltar calmly lifted his hand, palm outward toward Cris. Cris felt the air congeal around him, a buzz of energy filled his ears. He slowed and came to rest a meter in front of the Agent.

"How did you…?" Cris took a deep breath, feeling exposed floating in the middle of the dark room.

"In time, I'll teach you," Poltar replied. "The multiverse is filled with energy. Those of us who can feel the presence of the electromagnetism that surrounds us can learn to manipulate it. This allows us to perform incredible feats, such as levitating objects or focusing the energy around us into a concentrated sphere you can hold in the palm of your hand. Even thought is energy at its most basic level, which is where telepathy comes in. But the awareness goes beyond the physical world. For a rare few, we can detect—or even touch—subspace.

"The greater your connection to the unseen energy that surrounds you, the more control you will gain. There is a limit, of course, to how much energy a person can physically handle. We have tuned objects that can help us focus more, and we can work in teams. But alone, each person has a finite limit. This limit is a principle factor when determining an Agent's Course Rank. As part of the Course Test graduation exam, each Junior Agent is placed in a room with a single sphere made of a rare element that behaves like a quantum particle, simultaneously existing in this physical dimension and subspace. The Junior Agent is instructed to focus all the energy they can handle into the sphere, and we measure the input to determine the person's capacity. By the time most Junior Agents graduate, their abilities will be as fully developed as they will ever be in life. Though it can fluctuate for some, it's very uncommon. My responsibility is to teach you to focus the energy around you and control the maximum amount you can physically handle. Safely. Pushing too far or too fast can destroy a person. So we'll start small and work up from there."

Cris grinned. "Let's get started."

Poltar glided a couple meters away from Cris. "Close your eyes."

What's he going to do to me? Cris hesitated for a moment but complied.

"Can you tell where I am?" Poltar asked.

"I just saw you. You're right in front of me." *What kind of training is this?*

"Oh, am I?" Poltar said. The voice came from Cris' left.

Cris opened his eyes. Poltar had indeed moved to be three

meters off to his left. "That's a nice trick."

"Not a trick at all," the Agent countered. "If you were paying attention, you would have noticed that I moved."

Cris sighed. "How, exactly, would I be able to tell?"

"Every living thing has an electromagnetic signature. As someone sensitive to such things, you should be able to pick up on the presence of someone even without your eyes."

That's not very helpful instruction. Cris crossed his arms. "I don't feel much of anything while floating here in null."

"The null will make it easier for you to pick up on what's important, if you apply yourself. Come on, give it a shot."

With a sigh, Cris unfolded his arms and closed his eyes again. He tried to clear his mind and focus on the energy around him. After a few moments, he did start to feel a certain presence coming from the last place he had seen Poltar. *It's like the intuition Sedric always told me to use in combat.* He honed in on Poltar, judging his exact location. "Okay, I think I know what you mean." *Was I really using these abilities all along without knowing it?*

"I'm going to move around now," Poltar said. "Stay oriented in my direction."

"I'll try." Cris focused on Poltar's position. Initially, he didn't detect any movement, but slowly the energy seemed to shift. Cris started by turning only his head to track the movement, and then rotated his whole body. He moved back and forth several times, and then spun around entirely when he thought he sensed something behind him. The movements continued, becoming increasingly more erratic. It was difficult for Cris to follow at times, but whenever he started to feel lost, the presence seemed to come to a resting place. It was a fun game at first, but Cris started to feel bored with the exercise as it stretched on.

"You may open your eyes," Poltar said eventually.

Cris breathed a sigh of relief. *I couldn't take much more of that.* "How did I do?"

"You seem to be tracking well," Poltar replied. "I'd like to see how accurate you are at judging distance."

Cris tried to keep his boredom hidden. "All right."

"For reference, I'm currently three meters away," Poltar said.

This just keeps getting more thrilling. Cris closed his eyes and made note of how Poltar's presence felt at that distance. "Got it."

"Whenever I stop, call out how far away I am."

Cris sensed movement, and then Poltar stopped.

Cris thought for a moment. "Five meters." It was a guess, but he thought it was a reasonable attempt. There was movement again. Cris turned to his right as he tracked. "Seven meters." After the next movement, Poltar seemed closer. "Two meters."

Like the previous iteration, the exercise went on for far longer than Cris found engaging. *Why won't he tell me if I'm guessing right? I can't improve if I don't know what I'm doing wrong.*

"All right. Let's try something else," Poltar said, breaking the silence.

Finally. Cris opened his eyes.

Poltar moved toward the entrance door. He touched the wall, revealing a compartment. Inside, there were several chrome spheres. Poltar took four spheres from the compartment and closed it again. "These are probes. They will emit a minute electromagnetic pulse. I want you to identify the active probe."

That sounds like more of the same. "Okay," Cris acknowledged, a little disappointed. *I'm sure he has a reason for doing this, even if it doesn't make sense to me now.*

Poltar used telekinesis to distribute the probes around Cris at varying distances. "Point to the probe when it's active," he instructed.

Cris tried to locate the probes, but he couldn't detect anything other than Poltar himself. "I have no idea."

"It's subtle. Just give it your best guess."

Cris sighed inwardly. "Fine." He kept his eyes closed and started pointing in different directions—wherever gut instinct told him. He didn't consciously detect any signal from the probes, but following his initial reaction seemed reasonable.

Poltar gave no indication of how accurate he was, just made generic statements of encouragement every so often. Though Cris felt like he was randomly guessing, he continued.

"Okay, open your eyes," Poltar said, breaking the silence. "That's enough for a solid baseline."

"How'd I do?" Cris asked.

Poltar pulled out his handheld. "It's more important to judge your improvement than where you are now."

"Yeah, but—"

Poltar returned the handheld to his pocket. "It's been almost three hours. Want to break for lunch?"

He's smart to distract me from my question with food. "That would be great." Cris' stomach felt like it was about to eat itself, having only had two protein bars in the last day. *But I know better.* "I really am curious how I'm doing, though."

Poltar yielded. "You're a little more advanced than I anticipated. But there's a lot for me to teach you."

I hope we're almost done with the testing and can get to the fun parts. "I look forward to learning."

Poltar pulled Cris telekinetically toward the entrance door. He opened the hatch and they passed through the lock to reacclimate to gravity. Once outside, Poltar led the way to the central elevator that would take them up to the main Headquarters structure.

After some prodding, Cris got Poltar to explain the setup of the Headquarters structure during the elevator ride. The structure's eleven Levels were self-contained rings connected by a central shaft, and each served a distinct function. There were multiple floors on each Level, which could be accessed by stairways, but the central elevator shaft was the only means to access other Levels. The top Level was for Command and Medical. Agents were on the next three Levels, with Level 2 for the Primus Agents, the Level 3 for Sacon Agents and Level 4 for Trion Agents. Each of those Levels had Trainee quarters for the new students that were not yet assigned an official Agent class or area of specialization. There was also ample classroom space where the trainees in all ranks would convene, of which Cris was assured he'd see plenty in the coming years. Levels 5 through 9 were housing and training space for the Militia division. Level 10 contained primarily research labs and Engineering. The bottom ring of Headquarters, Level 11—where he had thus far spent most of his time—was suspended away from the rest of the structure. Since it was specifically for practicing telekinetic skills, Level 11 was outside of the subspace containment shell that surrounded the rest of the facility. Telekinesis could only be used sparingly in the rest of Headquarters, due to the natural dampening properties of subspace; it kept the trainees from getting out of hand.

Poltar took Cris back to Level 2, for the Primus class. There was a mess hall on every Level, Cris learned, except for the training area. Though Agents and trainees of any class were permitted into the other classes' mess halls, it was convention to use the facilities on the same Level as one's quarters unless invited to another—and such an invitation was always necessary for Militia members. The TSS culture dictated that at mealtime, Agents and trainees could come together in one place without the distinction of rank. When Cris walked into the mess hall, he was pleased to see Agents, Junior Agents, Initiates and Trainees sharing tables, though the clothing colors indicated that people still tended to stay within their own group more than not.

The Primus mess hall was large enough to accommodate four hundred people at the same time. Long tables with seats for ten people on each side filled the center of the room, and smaller tables dotted the perimeter. There were even some booths behind a short wall at the back of the room, for those seeking a more private conversation. The entire space was decorated with warm wood tones accented by gray and black fabrics, and potted plants stood out amongst the tables and the matte black floor. Along the right wall, people moved through a buffet line before selecting an open seat.

"Help yourself." Poltar gestured Cris toward the buffet.

Cris took a heaping tray of steaming meats, vegetables and bread with a few more cookies than would be considered appropriate. Poltar raised a skeptical eyebrow, but said nothing.

After surveying the room, Poltar led the way to one of the smaller tables along the left wall. Cris felt like everyone watched him pass by, not sure if it was because he was an unfamiliar face or that he was in the company of an Agent.

Cris dove into his meal, ravenous now that food was in front of him. Poltar had taken only a light lunch for himself and ate in silence across from Cris. While eating, Cris took in the people around him and tried to identify a pattern to the social framework. The more he observed, the more he realized that the co-mingling he thought he'd noticed when he first walked in was actually just a commander seated with their trainee group. Cris was the only individual below the rank of Junior Agent seated alone with an Agent.

"Why am I getting such unusual treatment?" Cris asked once he was most of the way through the plate of food.

Poltar tilted his head, questioning.

"I'm the only one here with a one-on-one mentor. I might be more advanced than some, but why not just throw me in with other new Trainees?"

"You have a lot of potential, Cris. Probably more than anyone else in this room. And now that you've begun to tap it, you need to be taught control before it overwhelms you."

Cris shook his head. "All of this has happened so fast. And

all this talk of 'potential'. I hardly feel like I know myself anymore."

"I heard about what happened at the spaceport—that kind of power is extraordinary. Most wouldn't be able to do those things without years of training. Without a foundation. Jumping right in at that level... well, the holes need to be filled in quickly. You could never get that in a normal training group."

"I just don't see how I'll ever fit in." *Yet again, I'm set apart. Is that just how it's destined to be for me?*

Poltar smiled. "Don't worry about that. I'll help you get control of your abilities, and then everyone will want to work with you. Who wouldn't want to have the best on their team?"

Cris shrugged. "I'm sure there's someone."

"Then they're shortsighted and ignorant. Anyone worth your time will respect you," Poltar said, looking Cris in the eye. "There is greatness in you. It's apparent to anyone who knows what to look for. They already see it in you." He surveyed the trainees and Agents throughout the room.

Cris looked about the room again. No uncertainty remained about whether he was being observed. People were engaged in their own conversations, but they kept glancing over at Cris. Darting glances, trying not to be caught. "What if I'm not what everyone thinks I am?"

"That kind of humility will get you far." Poltar eyed Cris' empty plate. "Ready to get back to it?"

There's no use fighting it. It's not my fault if they're wrong—I didn't ask for any of this. "Yes, sir."

‹ CHAPTER 9 ›

Cris felt like the walls were closing in on him. There was too much energy buzzing around him to concentrate.

A red cube hung in midair at eye level, spinning slowly. Poltar raised his hand and rotated his wrist, and the cube responded likewise. He lowered his hand, and the cube returned softly to the metal floor.

Cris let out his breath, not realizing he'd been holding it. "Is it always so intense?"

Poltar shook his head. "This room is an amplifier. It's designed to assist trainees like you. Even moderate exertion from a full Agent can seem like much more than it is."

There were four cubes on the ground in front of them, in ascending size. The smallest cube, green, was the size of Cris' fist. A yellow cube was twice that size, and the red Poltar had used for demonstration was about the size of his head. A blue cube, nearly a meter on each side, dwarfed the others.

"Clear your mind. Focus on the green cube. Command it." Poltar stepped to the back wall behind Cris, out of his view so he was not a distraction.

Cris stared at the cube. He squinted, willing it to obey his command. With clenched fists, he thought about it hovering in the air. Nothing happened. He sighed.

"You're trying too hard," Poltar said from behind him.

"I have no idea what I'm doing." *I threw a person across the hall without thinking about it, and now I can't do anything when I try.*

"Treat it as an extension of yourself," Poltar said. "Like a limb. When you're first learning to walk or write, you need to concentrate on what you're doing. Eventually, it will come without thinking."

Cris frowned. "I tr—"

"No, *really* clear your mind. Open yourself to knowing the cube. Feel it."

Letting go of his frustration, Cris breathed slowly and evenly—just as Sedric had taught him for combat. He envisioned a void, with the green cube as the only object in existence. He explored the cube, noting the way the light hit each of its planes. He evaluated its weight, the way it would feel to be held. *Rise.* The air began to buzz, vibrating. In Cris' mind, he saw a faint glow around the green cube, white light that seemed to shimmer. Ever so slowly, the cube began to lift off of the ground. *Rise!* The cube rose to a meter off the ground, a faint, glowing white column supporting it from the floor. Cris looked back to Poltar, excited, "I'm—!" The cube crashed to the floor. "Or, I did."

Poltar grinned. "Not bad at all." He leaned back against the metal wall. "Maintaining the levitation while talking is another lesson."

Cris smiled. "I've never seen anything like it. It was glowing."

Poltar nodded. "That was the electromagnetic field. Everyone seems to visualize it a little differently. I see yellow electric sparks, myself. Putting an image to it is common, helps with control."

"It just appeared."

"The mind is an amazing thing," Poltar said with a smile. "Now that you have a way to visualize the field, it should be easier to control."

"Huh." Cris stared at the cube, now seeming so plain and dull. *I don't know if I can ever look at things the same way again.*

"Why don't you try a larger one?" Poltar suggested.

"Okay." Cris focused on the yellow cube next. He cleared his mind again and made the yellow cube the center of the void in his mind. After several seconds, a white glow emerged, billowing into a column beneath the cube as it rose. The buzz of energy filled him, fueled him. He thirsted for more. Feeding the energy into the cube, he brought it up two meters off of the ground before slowly lowering it. *I did it!* He felt warm from the exertion, but invigorated.

"Good, and the next," Poltar instructed.

Cris concentrated. The red cube became surrounded by a white glow, but it didn't rise at first. Cris focused on it more intently, picturing it levitating in his mind, seeing the column pushing it upward. *Rise!* The cube inched upward, gaining speed as it rose. It overshot the height Cris had intended, nearly hitting the ceiling, and then descended quickly to the floor with a thud.

"Almost," Cris said sheepishly.

"Try the last one." Poltar nodded toward the largest blue cube. It was a significant jump in mass compared to the progression of the others.

Cris evaluated it dubiously. "Okay…" He focused on the blue cube, envisioning the white glow around it. The cube began to shudder as it was infused with energy. *Rise!* The cube quaked on the ground, rattling against the metal floor. Cris focused even more intently, seeing the energy flow into the cube. It glowed brighter, almost enough. He pressed harder. A corner of the cube rose off the ground, lifting—

"Stop! Don't strain yourself." Poltar put his hand on Cris' shoulder, and Cris felt the energy dissipate.

Cris nodded and let out a breath. *That felt incredible! The power…* He grinned at Poltar. "I was so close."

Poltar nodded, suddenly serious. "Go back to the yellow one."

After the difficulty of the blue cube, the mid-sized yellow object rose easily from the ground. He brought it to eye-level, and began slowly rotating it clockwise. The cube spun at a fixed height, steady. It was an island in the void of Cris' mind, surrounded by glowing energy. He felt like he could maintain the hold forever.

"Good, that's enough for today," Poltar stated, breaking the moment.

The cube faltered but didn't fall. Cris regained his serenity and lowered the cube slowly to the ground. The glow faded when the cube was at rest.

Cris rubbed his temples.

"Nicely done." Poltar clapped Cris on the shoulder. "How do you feel?"

"My head hurts. I feel wired." The buzz that had been in the air still hummed in his head. He wasn't sure if he was feeling it or hearing it.

"You should get in some physical exercise, too," Poltar added. "It's easy to get over-charged from telekinesis, until you know exactly how far to extend yourself. Exercise is a good release."

Cris nodded. Aside from any post-telekinesis benefits, there was no need to explain the importance of exercise while in artificial gravity. He had neglected his exercise routine for three weeks in the middle of his stint on the *Exler*, and the rapid atrophy he experienced was enough for him to never lapse again.

Poltar took Cris into a large open room with a track around the perimeter and weight equipment in the center. Only a few pieces of equipment were presently in use and several people were jogging around the track at various speeds. "You can use this track for now. A lot of trainees run laps in the residential halls, but we'll wait on that until you know your way around."

"All right." Cris' mind was still reeling, shocked by what he'd been able to do through telekinesis. The buzz had yet to subside.

"I'll leave you to it," Poltar said. "Run some laps and help yourself to the weights, if you feel up to it. We'll put together a formal physical training routine tomorrow. I'll meet you at the same time in the morning at your quarters."

"Yes, sir. Thank you." *I need to clear my head. Running laps is just what I need right now.*

"Great work today, Cris." Poltar hurried off.

Cris sighed. The entire day felt like a blur.

He jogged laps around the track, taking a leisurely pace for most of it but occasionally surging forward into a sprint. He noticed a few of the other runners were with a partner, but some were by themselves. *Finally, somewhere I don't stand out.* The buzz in his head lessened with each lap, eventually fading entirely. He thought about using some of the weight equipment but decided against it. Though the oppressive hum was gone, his mind was still racing, and he thought it best to just take some time to unwind back in his room.

Cris made his way back to the central elevator and rode it up to Level 2. Upon reaching the Primus level, he realized that all of the corridors branching from the central lobby looked the same. Some more prominent signage would be nice. He examined his options and ultimately picked the hallway that seemed the most familiar. Fortunately, his memory served him well and he traversed the remaining route to his quarters without making any wrong turns. When he reached his quarters, he placed his hand on the panel next to the entryway and the door slid open automatically for him.

"How was your first day?" Scott asked as Cris entered. He and Jon were lounging on the couch.

"Exhausting."

"Yeah, that tends to happen." Scott smiled. "So, what did

you go over today?"

Cris collapsed on the couch across from the Junior Agents. "First, he took me down to one of the spatial awareness chambers, I think they're called. He circled me while I had my eyes closed, and then had me sense some probes."

Scott and Jon looked at each other. "What did the probes look like?" Jon asked tentatively.

"Chrome, about the size of my fist."

The two Junior Agents shook their head and let out long breaths. "What then?" Scott questioned.

"We went into an empty room with some colored cubes on the floor. He had me try to lift them telekinetically," Cris went on, cautious.

"Could you?" Scott was expectant.

Cris swallowed. "I could only make the heaviest blue block shudder, but I didn't have too much trouble with the others. I held the yellow block for a few minutes."

Scott's jaw dropped open. Jon exclaimed, "That's impossible!"

Cris was taken aback. *Am I really that different?* He tried to sink into the couch, but he still felt completely vulnerable. "Is that bad? Poltar won't give me any specific feedback. He just keeps giving me different things to try."

Scott laughed. "Bad? It's incredible."

"Most are lucky if they can hold an object in suspension for a few seconds prior to being raised to Junior Agent," Jon added.

Cris' mouth went dry. *What am I?* "I didn't know."

"I can see why they took an interest in you," Scott said after a time.

Jon kept shaking his head.

Scott cleared his throat. "Hey, would you like to go to dinner with us?" Jon shot Scott a disapproving glare, but it was gone in an instant.

Cris had noticed the look but shrugged it off. "That would be great." *Was Poltar right? Will my power draw others to me?*

Cris felt much more confident walking into the mess hall with two Junior Agents rather than an Agent. His own light blue was not nearly as stark a contrast as it had been against the Agent's black. Scott led them to one of the larger communal tables and introduced Cris to some of the other Junior Agents, both men and women. The other Junior Agents were friendly and welcoming, though he did get some strange looks when Scott explained Cris' unconventional training situation. It soon seemed to be forgotten, and Cris became the center of attention, telling of his travels on the *Exler*. By the end of the evening, he was among old friends. He went to bed that night feeling content. *Maybe I do belong here.*

<>

The next morning, as he waited for Poltar to retrieve him for the day's studies, Cris finally took the opportunity to attend to some overdue business. After giving himself a little pep-talk, he sent a short note to his father's personal email letting him know that he was with the TSS and would not be coming home anytime soon. *He'll love that.*

Cris then turned his attention to the Mainframe. There was a seemingly endless wealth of information, even more than what he'd had access to on Tararia. It would take a lifetime to explore everything. He looked over entries about the TSS' spacecraft and navigation systems, but one specific item still stood out in his mind. *The Bakzen.* The main entry was frustratingly sparse and no more than he knew already—a rising enemy, living in the outskirts of explored space. "CACI, is there any more information on the Bakzen?"

"Restricted access. Additional clearance required," CACI replied.

Bomax. Looks like I won't be finding out any more for now.

He resumed his perusal of the other files until a video feed from the front door popped up. Poltar had arrived.

Cris went out to meet his instructor. "What are we doing today, sir?" he asked as he stepped into the hallway.

Poltar smiled. "First, we eat. Then, we get to work. I have it on good authority that you slacked on your workout last night, so we'll need to make up for it. I also need to see how you handle yourself in combat."

"I had a great teacher." *Sedric's lessons saved my life.*

"There's always more to learn."

"Will we be practicing any more telekinesis?"

Poltar nodded. "Absolutely."

<>   <>   <>

"He's been a very quick study, sir," Poltar said. "I know you want to keep his true identity hidden, but people will take notice of him all the same."

Banks paced across his office, weighing his options. "Many already are."

"So we should just advance him," Poltar urged.

"It goes completely against protocol." *Then again, so does everything about this.*

"I'm aware of that, sir. I just think anything less would be an unnecessary delay. You instructed me to move him through as quickly as possible, and, in my professional opinion, he'll be ready in four months."

Banks stopped his pacing in front of his desk. He slumped down on the edge, torn. "Moving him straight to Junior Agent will be an administrative nightmare. But, it's my duty to take your recommendation under advisement. We'll need to conduct a formal evaluation."

Poltar nodded. "Of course, sir."

"Thank you for the update. You're doing great work."

"Thank you, sir." Poltar bowed his head.

"Dismissed."

Poltar bowed again, a little deeper, and left.

Banks rubbed his eyes. *Advanced to Junior Agent after four months?* Unheard of and unorthodox, perhaps, but there was no more time to waste.

PART 3: FULFILLMENT

◄   CHAPTER 10   ►

"Come on, just one more lap."

Cris eyed Scott with open skepticism. His lungs and legs burned.

"It's good for you!" Scott grinned.

Cris had always thought he was in good shape, but Scott had proved to be a demanding training partner. Even after more than three years of training together as Junior Agents, Cris couldn't figure out where all the energy came from. "*One* more."

"That's the spirit!" Scott took off down the hallway.

Cris willed his legs to move again and followed, centering his mind to block out the aching and burning he felt everywhere.

Scott set the pace at a fast jog, following the corridor that looped around the perimeter of the Primus residential wings on Level 2 in the Headquarters structure. The loop was approximately five kilometers, which seemed even longer by the end of an already exhausting workout. Despite the cool temperature, Cris was hot and slick with sweat. His t-shirt was off, tucked into the back of his pants, to let the air cool his bare chest and back. Scott ran shirtless a few paces ahead of him, showing no intent of slowing down. Cris urged himself onward.

They neared the halfway point in the lap. *Almost there.* Cris' legs and lungs ached for relief.

A group of fellow Junior Agents were sprawled out on the floor of the hallway up ahead, resting their backs against the walls. Such impromptu study groups were a common sight on their afternoon jogs. Cris picked his way carefully through the first sets of legs sticking out into his path, weaving around other bystanders blocking his way. He was so focused on avoiding the obstacles that he didn't realize Scott had stopped.

"Hold up, Cris." Scott returned his attention to a pretty blonde with short hair and bright blue eyes who was sitting on the floor with some other Junior Agents. Scott crouched down to talk with her more closely. She laughed.

Cris sighed. *Here we go again.* He untucked his shirt from his pants, using it wipe the sweat from his face.

Scott looked over at Cris and then back at the blonde. She nodded vigorously.

Oh no. Cris looked around for a quick escape, but it was too late.

"Cris, come here." Scott waved him over.

Cris reluctantly complied, trying to control his panting breath and racing heart.

"So Cris," Scott said as Cris approached, "this is Marsie Katz. We were thinking it would be fun to go on a double date tomorrow."

Double date? "That would be something…"

"Great!" Scott grinned at Marsie.

"I'm looking forward to it," someone said from below Cris in a gentle female voice.

Cris startled backward. Her back had been to him, but she now twisted around to look at him. Her long, dark-brown hair was pulled up into a ponytail, leaving the ends in a loose wave about her shoulders. Bright hazel-green eyes that had begun to glow with bioluminescence drew him in. She was by far the most beautiful woman he'd ever seen, but there was something else—he felt instantly connected to her. His breath caught as they locked eyes, and he felt like his heart had stopped beating. Her lips parted in a sweet, genuine smile, and he felt suddenly at ease with her while still being overcome with anxious anticipation.

"Hi," Cris finally stammered, thankful that his cheeks were already flushed from the run.

"Hi," she replied, taking him in. Cris couldn't quite read her expression, but it seemed favorable. "I'm Kate."

"Nice to meet you," Cris managed to get out, still lost in her eyes.

"Well this will be great fun tomorrow!" Scott jumped to his feet. "Later, ladies." He jogged a couple of steps. "Come on, Cris, time to get back to it."

"Bye," Cris said, pulling himself from Kate. He took a few steps and glanced over his shoulder, seeing that she was still watching him go.

Wow. Cris didn't feel any of the burn in the last two kilometers.

<><>

Cris relaxed on the couch, thankful for the magical healing properties of a hot shower. Scott emerged from the bathroom, toweling his hair.

"So I have to admit," Scott began, "that it really wasn't fair of me to drag you into a double date like that."

Cris' heart skipped a beat, thinking about Kate again. "It's fine, I know how you are."

"No, not like that." Scott screwed up his face, searching for words. "Here's the thing…"

"What?"

"Uh…" Scott took a deep breath. "She's… High Dynasty."

Cris' mouth dropped open involuntarily. "Wait, *what*?"

"Man, I'm sorry. Like I said… Look, Marsie is her roommate and they're good friends. Some people are kind of wary about hanging with Kate because of who she is, and Marsie wanted to give her a chance to get out, so we thought a double date would be good. And you and I are friends, so—"

Cris felt sick. "Which Dynasty, Scott?" *Fok, who is she?*

"Vaenetri. She's Katrine Vaenetri."

Cris let out a shaky breath. *Thank the stars, not a relative! But Vaenetri, of all the families. After Tristen and her sister...* "That's... unexpected."

Scott sat down on the couch, wringing his towel. "I know, I know. I'll make it up to you. I'm just asking for one night."

"It's fine." *Kate Vaenetri...*

"Fine? Fine! Great." Scott leaped to his feet. "Yes, it's going to be just fine."

Cris raised a quizzical eyebrow. "Are you okay?"

"Yes! Of course." Scott bit his lip. He sat back down. "How are you so calm about all of this? A *Lady* from a *High Dynasty* and you're 'fine'? I'm kind of freaking out here. How do you even talk to someone like that?"

Cris laughed inwardly. "High Dynasty or not, they're still just people. They're not all that different."

"Hah! Right." Scott rose to his feet, tossing his towel over his shoulder. "I knew I was bringing along the right guy." Scott went into his room, muttering something under his breath.

Cris sighed, and it turned into a chuckle. Even coming all the way to the TSS couldn't get him out of a dinner with an eligible High Dynasty bachelorette.

<>

The day went by far too slowly. Cris had spent the whole night and following day thinking about Kate, despite himself. She didn't exude the elitist air that he'd come to expect from anyone born into the High Dynasties, and he was anxious to see if that perception held true once he got to know her. After finishing up his classes for the day, he was finally free to return to his quarters and prepare for his double date. *Excited for date night?* He sighed. *What's happened to me?*

Cris went about showering and dressing in his quarters, the

only home he'd known since coming to the TSS. After TSS command had decided to promote Cris directly to Junior Agent, he'd stayed in the same quarters he was first assigned with Scott and Jon. Jon had recently graduated, and like many new Agents had been sent on assignment to Jotun in the outer colonies. They had never been assigned a fourth roommate, so it was temporarily just Scott and Cris. Scott had learned to take full advantage of the arrangement, often kicking Cris out for several hours so he could engage in more private activities with his female companions.

Once dressed in the same dark blue t-shirt and pants that now comprised his entire wardrobe, Cris went out into the common area. Scott emerged from his room at the same time.

"Ready?" Scott asked.

"As I'll ever be."

Cris and Scott made their way to the Primus mess hall. As they approached, Cris saw that Marsie and Kate were waiting for them outside the main door. Both women wore the standard dark blue tank tops that normally served as undershirts for the women's uniform, with a scoop neckline tapering into thin straps that criss-crossed their backs. Their pants were more form-fitting than the men's uniform, slim down to their knees and flared slightly around the cuff covering their boots. Marsie had added some curl to her short blonde hair, and Kate now wore hers in a loose braid.

I've never seen someone so naturally stunning, Cris thought to himself as he admired Kate. She smiled in greeting when she saw him, and he felt his heart flutter. *Gah! Stay cool.*

Marsie gave Scott a hug when he walked up to her, and they exchanged a playful glance.

"Shall we eat?" Scott said, gesturing toward the large doorway into the mess hall.

They loaded their trays and selected a booth along the back wall. Scott slid in next to Marsie, leaving Cris the spot next to

Kate. *You can do this!* He sat down next to her, trying to judge an appropriate distance apart.

When they started eating, Cris noticed that Kate still followed the proper etiquette instilled in all members of the High Dynasties, so he was especially diligent in maintaining the more casual mannerisms he'd picked up aboard the *Exler* and from those around him at the TSS. As best he could, he tried to walk the line between politeness and commonplace. *Something as simple as how I hold my fork could give me away to a trained eye. If she's interested in me, I want it to be because of who I am as a person, not for my pedigree.*

They engaged in idle small talk as they ate. Some big tests later that week, wish lists for their internship assignments that would be announced any day. Cris was careful to keep his mind guarded against any potential telepathic probe.

"Cris, here," Scott ventured after a time, "spent a year on a freighter touring the galaxy before joining the TSS. I think he's seen more than any of us."

"How fun!" Marsie exclaimed.

"What was your favorite part about it?" Kate asked.

"How I got a different perspective on life. Saw how others lived," Cris reflected.

"I've appreciated that about the TSS," Kate said. "There are so many people from different backgrounds here. My life back home was so sheltered by comparison."

"It's hard to get the big picture from one vantage, no matter what it may be." *I had arguably the best education available, but what I've learned since leaving Tararia has been far more valuable.*

"So, Cris, where are you from originally?" Marsie inquired.

Here we go... Cris had his back-story down, but it was something else entirely to recite it in front of another High Dynasty member. He glanced at Kate, before proceeding. "I'm from Tararia, the Third Region. Sieten." Kate looked over in interest, but Cris didn't detect any recognition or suspicion. *She doesn't expect to see me as High Dynasty, so she doesn't.*

"I've never been there, but I hear it's beautiful," Marsie replied. "I would have tried to get into the University there if I hadn't been recruited by the TSS."

"Yes, it's quite lovely." *I wish I still had the view from my bedroom window.*

"Do you miss it?" Kate asked.

Cris looked down at his plate. *That's such a loaded question.* "Sometimes, but it wasn't the life I wanted."

Kate nodded. "I know exactly what you mean." She looked down at her own plate, seeing past it.

She does? Cris saw a new somberness in her softly glowing eyes. *Is she like me?*

"Sorry, I didn't know it was such a touchy subject!" Marsie said with a little laugh.

"Oh, don't mind them," Scott said, putting his arm around Marsie. "Homesickness can get everyone down sometimes."

Cris forced a smile. "There's way too much going on here to miss home much."

"Too true!" Scott said, squeezing Marsie. "Gorgeous women, cutting-edge tech and free food—what else do you really need?"

Everyone rolled their eyes in exasperation, but they knew there was truth in his statement. They were in the midst of one of the good times in life, and they had enough perspective to recognize it.

The Junior Agents finished their meal between more light conversation and laughter, enjoying each other's company. As the evening went on, Scott and Marsie inched closer together and talked quietly to each other so that Cris and Kate couldn't overhear. Eventually, when there was a lull in the conversation, Marsie leaned in and whispered in Scott's ear.

"We should probably get going," Scott announced.

"This has been a lot of fun," Marsie added. "It was great to meet you, Cris."

"You too," Cris replied.

"Well, you two have fun the rest of tonight," Scott said as they got up. "Try to stay out of trouble." He winked at Cris.

Cris sighed and shook his head when they were out of earshot. "That guy…"

Kate smiled. "Marsie is no better. They were made for each other."

What do I do now that I'm alone with her? "You're under no obligation to spend the rest of the evening with me," Cris blurted out.

Kate shook her head. "Nonsense. I'm enjoying your company." She scoped out the buffet from afar. "I could really use some dessert."

"I'm game."

They procured some chocolate mousse and returned to the booth, sitting across from each other.

"So, Kate, I'm sure you get this all the time, but I have to ask. How did you come to join the TSS? As far as I know, it's rare for anyone from a High Dynasty to come train here, especially beyond the first year." Cris took a bite of the mousse; not quite as good as the Sietinen private chef's, but still delicious.

Kate sighed. "I'm… a bit of an anomaly. I have an older brother, who's heir, and two older sisters. Most High Dynasties only have one or two successors. So, as a fourth child, I'm of little consequence."

"Are you close with your siblings?"

She shrugged. "Not really. They were adults by the time I was born. I'm twenty years younger than my closest sister."

Cris just about choked on his mousse, but was able to hide it. *Twenty years younger…* That meant there were no children in between Kate and Krista, Tristen's betrothed. It was too big of a coincidence for Kate to be Cris' age. He swallowed. "I know what it's like growing up alone." *Even after what happened, they still wanted to unite the two Dynasties.*

"So, at any rate," Kate went on, "when my abilities started to emerge, it was decided that I could come train here. There wasn't any reason for me to stay on Tararia."

I was gone, and they knew it. "I hope you feel like you made the right choice." *I know I did.*

"Yes, I do. How about you? What brought you here?"

Cris picked his words carefully. "I didn't get along with my parents. I think my father actively disliked me. My mother, on the other hand, barely acknowledged my existence. They especially disapproved of me embracing my abilities. So, as soon as I could, I left home. I met Thom, the captain of the *Exler*, on my first day out on my own, and he took me in. I got really lucky."

"I heard the TSS actually tracked you down to recruit you. And that you trained privately with an Agent when you first got here."

Cris opened his mouth to reply, but didn't know what to say. He shrugged it off. "We're all in the same place now."

Kate looked at him thoughtfully with eyes that contained wisdom beyond her years. "I've never met anyone quite like you," she said. "You act so casual, but you have a certain… poise."

"I'm me. It's just the way I am."

Kate smiled. "I like it."

They both looked down at their empty bowls.

"What now?" Cris asked. It was still a little early to go back to his quarters, if he knew Scott's habits.

"Let's go up to the spaceport," Kate suggested, excitement in her eyes. "It's been too long since I've seen the stars."

"Okay," Cris agreed, ready to follow her lead anywhere she wanted.

Kate took Cris' hand and led him to the central elevator that would take them on the long ride to the surface of the moon outside of Headquarters. They didn't have the clearance to take a transport vessel up to the dock with the TSS fleet, but they could go as far as the terminal on the surface.

The terminal was all but deserted, and they went over to one of the expansive windows that curved in a half-dome overhead, providing an unobstructed view of the starscape beyond.

"I love coming here," Kate said, staring out. They leaned against the railing in front of the window. "It all looks so different from space. You can't get a view like this on Tararia."

"No, you certainly can't," Cris replied. He could never tire of gazing out into the impressive blackness of space with its amazing spectrum of stars.

Kate inched closer to Cris. After a moment, he took the hint and put his arm around her. She relaxed against him. Nothing else mattered with her next to him like that. He was completely at peace. He had no idea how long they stood together, but he savored every moment.

A wave of tiredness washed over Cris. He checked the time on his handheld: 24:13. *How is that even possible?* It was past curfew, though that was rarely enforced for Junior Agents. "We should get back." He reluctantly unfurled himself from Kate.

Kate checked her own handheld. "I had no idea it was so late!"

"It's probably safe for me to go back to my quarters now."

Kate stifled a yawn. "Yes, I should think so."

They took the central elevator down to the Primus level and walked back to Kate's quarters, her arm linked around Cris'. *I could walk like this forever.*

"I had a great time tonight," Kate said when they were outside her door. "I hope we can see more of each other."

"Me too."

She looked up expectantly at Cris, but he hesitated, not sure what to do.

"Well, good night." Cris smiled and turned to go, his heart

pounding in his ears.

"Aren't you going to kiss me goodnight?"

He turned back to look at her. She gazed into his eyes, searching. "I didn't want to presume. You are a Lady, after all," he said.

"Consider the invitation extended." She took a step forward.

Cris swallowed. Coaching about girls hadn't been a part of any of his training. *I have no idea what I'm doing.* He let instinct take over, cupping Kate's face in his hand and drawing her to him.

Their lips met, sending a tingle through Cris' entire body. Kate placed her arms around his neck and pulled him closer. Despite his inexperience, Cris felt at once comfortable with her, following her every cue. She wanted more, but he pulled back slowly from the kiss. "Good night." He kissed her again lightly, lingering just long enough.

‹ CHAPTER 11 ›

"How was your date?" Scott asked as soon as Cris emerged from his room in the morning.

Cris grinned, in spite of himself. "It was good."

Scott laughed. "Someone is smitten!"

"Well, I wouldn't go that far," Cris said, trying to sound casual. *She's the most incredible person I've ever met. I didn't know someone like her even existed.*

"Uh huh." Scott didn't seem convinced. "When are you seeing her next?"

"We didn't make any plans yet." *Stars, I hope it's soon.*

"Marsie sent me a message last night saying that Kate was gushing about you."

Really? "I'm glad she had a good time."

"By the look on your face, the feeling was mutual."

Cris shrugged it off. *Stay cool. It was only one date. But stars! It was great.*

"Anyway, I'm glad it worked out." Scott pulled out his handheld and checked it. "Hey, I have to check in with the lab. I'll see you later."

"Have a good one." Cris rubbed his eyes. *Yes, it was a wonderful night, but we were up far too late to now be awake at this hour.* He suppressed a yawn.

Cris took a quick shower before heading over to the mess hall for breakfast. He got his tray of food and was about to sit down at an empty table when he spotted Kate eating alone. She was reading something projected from her handheld. *Do I go over to her?* As he was trying to decide what to do, she looked up from the text and smiled at him. After a moment, she waved him over. *Okay, that answers it.*

"Good morning," she greeted as he approached. She collapsed her handheld and put it away in her pants pocket.

"Good morning." Cris took a seat across from her, instantly energized in her presence. *How could I miss her so much after just a few hours?*

Kate set down her fork. "I wasn't sure if I should call you over or not. You don't have to sit here if—"

"No, I'm glad you did. I didn't want to interrupt you."

Kate smiled. "Good. I was afraid you might take it as me being too clingy, or something."

Cris chuckled. "Not at all." He took a bite of potato scramble from his plate. "It's good to see you again."

Kate blushed slightly. "You too." She took a couple bites from her own plate. "I had a great time last night."

"Me too."

They resumed eating in silence.

Cris kept his eyes on his plate. The quiet was awkward. *Maybe it was a bad idea to come over here? I remember Scott mentioning something about a waiting period between dates...*

"I'd like to get to know you," Kate said suddenly.

Startled, Cris looked up and their eyes locked. The awkwardness melted away.

"It felt right, last night," Kate continued. "I know Scott and Marsie are just fooling around, but there seemed to be a real connection with us."

And I still feel it now. Cris couldn't look away. "I agree. I'd very much like to get to know you more."

Kate smiled. "Good." She tore away and looked down for a moment. She cleared her throat. "Now, you said you were from

Seiten, right?"

Cris' breath caught. *Stars! Exactly how well do I want her to know me right away?* "Yeah, from right outside the city." *Do I come clean?*

"And you said you grew up alone. Only child?"

"Yes. Well, sort of. I had a brother who died in an accident before I was born." *If she makes the connection between Tristen and her sister...*

Kate's brow furrowed with sympathy. "That must have been difficult for your family."

Cris breathed an inward sigh of relief. *She doesn't suspect me. Or at least doesn't want to admit it.* "It was tough growing up in a shadow. Aside from my parents disapproving of my abilities, that's the other key reason I chose to leave Tararia." *I want to tell her everything, but I need to know that she cares about me, not who I am.*

"I can relate." Kate withdrew in thought for a moment. "Anyway, what interests you? What do you enjoy studying?"

Right now, you interest me more than anything. "I love flying. Any chance I have to get in the fighter jets is welcome. On the more academic side, recently I've been diving into the deepest layers of subspace mechanics."

"Scott mentioned you had a knack for navigation."

I can't escape the family business entirely. "Yes, admittedly, much of the subspace studying has navigation applications. I did work as a Navigator before joining the TSS, so it's a familiar subject. But, it's something I'm good at, more than something I enjoy."

"I know what you mean. That's like me with telecommunications systems, because of my family. I can construct a holographic projector from parts, but I'd much rather help plan a battle strategy." She grinned.

Of course. She was groomed in the operations of VComm, just as I was groomed to take over SiNavTech. "I second your sentiment about battle strategy. Agent Reisar's class was incredible."

Kate's eyes lit up. "It was! When you took it, did he give you that lecture on using phantom subspace jumps?"

"Yes! That was so awesome. I mean, I'd hope to never find myself in that situation, but—" Cris was interrupted by a loud chirp from his handheld. "Sorry." He reached into his pocket to silence the device.

A moment later, Kate's handheld made the same chirp. She groaned and pulled it out from her pocket to look at the message. She frowned. "I've been summoned."

Cris examined his own handheld. The message read: "Proceed to Junior Agent Lounge JAP-271C." He showed Kate.

"Same for me," she confirmed.

Are we in trouble? Cris took one final bite of breakfast. "I guess we should go."

They bussed their table and walked together to the lounge. A handful of other Junior Agents were already there, including Scott. "Any idea why we're here?" Cris asked.

"No," Scott replied.

"Internships?" Kate speculated.

Scott shrugged. "Maybe."

After five more minutes, a dozen Primus Junior Agents were gathered in the middle of the room, including Marsie and some other common acquaintances from various classes. Everyone chatted amongst themselves, throwing out increasingly far-fetched theories about the meeting.

The door slid open again and everyone immediately fell silent when a figure dressed in black entered. After a moment, Cris recognized the man as Lead Agent Nilaen. He was one of the oldest Agents Cris had encountered, with almost fully gray hair. However, he still held himself with the same regality as his younger counterparts. Cris had never interacted with him directly, but he knew his reputation for fair issue resolution and attention to detail.

Nilaen beamed at the crowd. "I'm sure you've all had time to theorize why you have been gathered here." The Junior Agents nodded. "Well, I'm pleased to tell you that the day has finally arrived. Your internship assignments await you."

The Junior Agents looked to each other with anxious anticipation.

Kate shot Cris a smug look. "I knew it." She clasped her hands. "Please, be somewhere warm."

Nilaen checked his handheld. "The details of the assignments have been transferred to your accounts. Good luck." He departed as the Junior Agents scattered to review the assignments with their friends.

"Let's see what we got," Cris said to Kate. They pulled up the files on their handhelds. Cris scanned through the information. It seemed like a straightforward assignment on a pleasant planet, but the subject matter was pretty low on his wish list. *Great. I have to deal with diplomats.* He looked to Kate. "What did you get?"

"Valdos III," Kate replied with disdain. "This looks awful! Just completely… boring."

"How so?"

She continued flipping through the file, looking more distraught the more she read. "Well, their flag is solid beige. I think that says everything."

Cris gave her a sympathetic smile. "I'm sure it will be fine."

Kate sighed loudly. "Easy for you to say, since you won't be stuck there for the next year. Where did you end up?"

She won't like this. "Marilon II. Fairly temperate climate and mountainous landscape—pretty picturesque, actually. But, it would seem the Districts don't know how to play nice with each other and they need a mediator." *I'll be stuck in the role of politician after all.*

"Let me see." Kate grabbed his handheld and brought up a

holographic projection of the planet's landscape. Towering trees stood out among dramatic rocky cliffs. A modern metropolis was nestled in the foothills with a clear blue river bisecting the city. "You have to be kidding!" She shoved the handheld back at him.

"To be fair, I'll probably spend all of my time in conference rooms," Cris pointed out.

"At least you'll have something to look at out the window." Kate pulled up a holographic display of her own location on her handheld.

Cris wanted to laugh, but held back. The capital city of Valdos III was flat, featureless and bland. The inhabitants all appeared to wear loose-fitting clothes in an awful shade of gray-tan, giving the entire civilization a completely monotone appearance. "It's... quaint? And it looks like you did get your wish for somewhere warm."

Kate's eyes narrowed into a malicious glare. "Don't even try."

"Hey, I didn't make the assignments!" Cris held up his hands in self-defense.

"Someone doesn't look happy," Scott said from behind Cris.

Perfect timing! Cris turned to his friend. "Not every planet has high tourist appeal. How did you fair?"

"Meh, fine," Scott replied. "I'll be managing supply distribution on one of the recently settled colony worlds in the border territories. You?"

"Diplomatic relations on Marilon II," Cris told him, trying to block out Kate's seething stare.

"How is this fair?" Kate exclaimed, taking ahold of Cris' handheld again and directing it toward Scott.

Scott looked it over. "Hmm, that's not a typical internship assignment. Lucky you."

"I'm sure I'll be miserable in my own way." *If only they knew how much I loathed these sorts of political dealings.*

"Fair enough," Scott said. "Be nice, Kate. At least you'll get to practice advanced telekinesis on Valdos III—I've heard it's one of the only planets where it's integral to their culture."

Kate placed her handheld back in her pocket and crossed her arms. "Lovely." She sighed. "What about Marsie?"

Scott shook his head. "I don't know. She muttered something about 'may as well be going to a convent' before storming off."

Every assignment is deliberate, designed to address our greatest weaknesses. I guess we're finding out what parts of ourselves we need to improve. "Well, we have a couple months to get used to everything before we ship out."

"Very true," Scott agreed. "I need to start this reading."

"Yes, I should do the same," Kate said. "I'm sure there's *some* redeeming quality about this place. I may as well know what it is."

"That's the spirit," Cris said. "Catch up later?"

"Sure. I'll message you." She smiled at him, all of the discontent from earlier forgotten.

Cris smiled back and nodded.

When they were several meters from the lounge, Scott shook his head. "You two are already sickening together. I'm regretting setting you up."

"You're just jealous."

Scott rolled his eyes. "When you're playing with your grandkids, remember I was the one who made it all possible."

Cris gave him a playful shove.

Scott grinned and leaped ahead of Cris. "And name your firstborn after me!" He took off in a sprint down the hallway.

I should expect nothing less from him. When Cris eventually arrived at his quarters, Scott had already retreated into his room. Cris settled onto his own bed so he could begin the arduous review of the mission details for his internship. He was about to start reading when he noticed an unread email notification.

His stomach knotted when he saw the message in his inbox. *Ugh, not again.* It was from his father. The subject was simply: "Checking in." Cris groaned and deleted the message. He had received dozens of similar emails and video recordings over the last three years. All of them said the same thing, even though the packaging varied: "Your training with the TSS is pointless. You have no future there. Come home to where you belong."

Except, I don't belong on Tararia. And now I have Kate here. They can't argue about a High Dynasty match. He flipped to the internship brief. *This is the last step. Soon I'll be an Agent. Kate and me, together as Agents. We'd be unstoppable.* He couldn't picture a brighter future.

◄   CHAPTER 12   ►

After reviewing the details for his internship, Cris was convinced Banks was playing a cruel joke on him. Mediating political negotiations would be Cris' version of a nightmare.

To make matters worse, the more time he spent with Kate in the ensuing weeks, the more the reality of their impending time away sunk in. They would be apart for at least six months, maybe a year. *Already I can't imagine being away from her. Why couldn't we have met after we got back?*

Knowing their time was limited, they saw each other almost every day at meals. Occasionally over the next few weeks, there were opportunities to spend an evening together, but most of that time was spent studying. Still, Cris was happy to get any time he could with Kate, even if it was just sitting in the same room.

One such evening, Cris and Kate were working on their tablets in the common room of Cris' quarters. Scott was away for a few hours completing a project in an engineering lab down on Level 10.

Kate looked up from her reading. "Do you ever stop to think about just how rare we are?"

"What do you mean?" Cris asked from the adjacent couch.

"There are forty-two trainees going on internships this year," Kate said. "According to this article, there used to be hundreds in each cohort."

Hundreds of Agents graduating at one time? "What changed?"

"The article doesn't go into it." Kate set down her tablet on the coffee table. "I can't read any more today."

"I second that." Cris stretched and set down his own tablet. It was late and his eyes were glazing over.

Kate came over to Cris' couch and cuddled up next to him. "It makes you wonder, though."

"What do you think happened?"

Kate thought for a moment. "I bet people with abilities are too scared to come forward. The TSS comes across some by chance and will recruit them, but thousands—maybe hundreds of thousands—are probably hiding their abilities. Without any training, all of that talent just gets suppressed and ignored until it may as well not exist at all."

Like my father. And Tristen, in his attempt to be the perfect son. "That very easily could have happened to you."

Kate nodded, pensive. "I was pretty lucky to be a fourth child, I suppose. Otherwise, I would have been pulled into the responsibilities of the Dynasty rather than being allowed to train with the TSS."

"Your siblings weren't so fortunate."

Kate frowned. "If my sisters and brother have abilities, they certainly never let on."

She doesn't know... Cris swallowed. "Abilities come in Generations, Kate. If you have them, then they do, too."

"Are you sure? It seems strange that they never would have said anything."

Cris carefully composed his response. *Kate could very well be the ally I've always hoped to find. But I can't reveal my full hand yet.* "The Priesthood's influence is strongest on Tararia, especially with the High Dynasties who are supposed to be leaders and set example for others. How bad would it look for dynastic members to publicly display the abilities the Priesthood tries to denounce?"

Kate looked sick. "Stars! No wonder they let me come here… I always thought they were letting me do what I wanted, but maybe they just wanted me out of the way."

"I'm sure that wasn't the only reason." *I know exactly how she feels… Realizing your family wishes you would blend in, just like them.*

"Now I don't know what to believe." She looked away.

Cris rubbed her shoulder. "I'm sorry, I didn't mean to upset you."

She shook her head. "No, it's not you. I just hate the idea of being lied to."

Cris bit his lip and swallowed. *I haven't been completely honest with her, either.*

"I just never thought about it before," Kate continued. "Sometimes I feel like I was living under a rock. You must have heard all sorts of things in your travels—the kind of things they'd never talk about on Tararia or here within the TSS."

And, consequently, I came up with a lot of crazy notions. "I did come across some really disgruntled people. Everything might seem fair and balanced in the inner colonies, but it's completely different in the border territories. Out there, people would rather the central government not exist."

Kate's jaw dropped. "No Priesthood or High Dynasties?"

"I know, it surprised me, too."

Her brow furrowed. "What do they have against them?"

Aside from everything? "I think it's more that they feel they don't have a voice. The services provided by the High Dynasties are supposed to be for the good of the people—providing the necessities for life and prosperity. But in reality, the Dynasties' companies are complete monopolies and the average person has no say in the type of service they receive or how much it costs."

Kate nodded. "Which is why the Priesthood provides oversight."

"But what does the Priesthood really know? Their decision-makers live a luxurious life on Tararia just like any member of the High Dynasties. Even if they have advisors on other worlds, decisions will always be skewed in favor of the majority leaders."

"And you think there's a better way?" Kate asked.

Cris shrugged. "I don't know, maybe. It just doesn't seem right the way it is."

Kate tilted her head back to look up at him. "What would you propose?"

"I'm probably not the best person to ask…" *This could be my chance to find out if she really does think like me or is content with the way things are on Tararia.*

"No, I'm curious," Kate insisted. "What do you have in mind?"

All right, let's see what she thinks of this. "Make the Dynasties' corporations public. Their operations would be dictated by the vote of the populace."

Kate stared at Cris, stunned. "Whoa. That's…"

Cris grinned in attempt to downplay the radical proposition. "I know. Like I said, I'm probably not the best person to ask."

"The Priesthood would never go along with that," Kate continued after a pause.

"Of course not."

"Wait." She caught Cris' eye. *"Are you suggesting to remove the Priesthood from power?"* she asked telepathically.

Cris looked down and closed his mind to her. *This is a dangerous conversation. The Priesthood already tried to kill me once.* "Never mind."

Kate reached up to turn Cris' face toward her. "Do you think it would be possible?"

Cris let out a slow breath. "I've thought about it. Under the right circumstances, it could be done."

"How?"

I didn't mean to go this deep now, but she does seem

intrigued. "It would require a majority vote from the High Dynasties."

"I guess." Kate let out a little laugh. "Like they'd ever agree."

"If you could convince your family, that would be one vote. It would just take three more." *Sietinen would provide another, once I'm in charge.*

"Right. I can just say 'pretty please' and they'll relinquish control."

Maybe this was a mistake. "Forget it. I'm clueless when it comes to politics. Maybe I'll learn something on my internship." He leaned down to kiss Kate.

She kissed him back but was still distracted. "It would take years to get the alliances in place for that kind of overthrow."

Cris hesitated. *Do I let this continue?* "Probably a generation or two."

Kate nodded. "Even if the Dynasties went along with it, what about the financial infrastructure and biomedical? The Priesthood plays an important role as a neutral third-party."

I'm not sure how neutral they really are. "The function would need to be replaced under the new system, of course. I'm far from having all the solutions at this point. I just know I see a problem with the way things are presently."

"It is tough to support the Priesthood when they don't want people like us to exist," Kate murmured.

"My sentiment exactly."

Kate looked distant, then her face softened and she laughed. "What are we doing? We're going to be TSS Agents. This isn't our problem to worry about."

Cris forced a laugh. "You are absolutely right. I tried to warn you about me." He grinned, both as a cover and out of genuine happiness for discovering he had more in common with Kate than he ever dreamed. *We could really do it. We could lead a revolution together.*

"I never thought of myself as the type to hang out with the

bad crowd."

Cris pulled her in for a kiss, wrapping his arms around her. He parted for a moment. "I'm a rebel, what can I say?"

She ran her fingers through his hair. "You're going to cause so much trouble on Marilon…"

"I bet you'll be just as bad by the time you come home, after all that time in one of the only places that doesn't share the anti-telekinesis sentiment of the central worlds."

Kate made a playful frown. "Between your influence and that, I'm doomed."

"Try not to think of it as 'doomed'—more, 'enlightened'."

"Uh huh…" She repositioned on his lap. "And I take it you're going to help me continue preparing for this internship?"

"Naturally. I still have a few more weeks to get you talking crazy like me."

"With so little time, is talking really the way you want to spend it?" She kissed Cris' neck.

A warm tingle ran through him. "I'm open to other suggestions." *The revolution can wait.*

<> <> <>

Banks was reviewing some weekly reports from his commanding Agents when his desk lit up with an incoming message notification. He looked at the caller. *The Priesthood always has impeccable timing.* He composed his face and accepted the call as he rose from his desk.

"Hello," Banks greeted in Old Taran while he stepped toward the viewscreen. "To what do I owe the honor of your call?"

The Priest did not look like he was in the mood for pleasantries. "How are matters progressing?"

Straight to business, as usual. "Everything is on track."

The Priest glowered. "So you keep saying, but we have yet to see any results."

"These things take time. We can't push too hard without drawing suspicion. You'll have what you want in a few short years, I assure you."

"Years?"

Banks was steadfast. *Your decisions are what got us in this position.* "We'd be done by now if you hadn't abandoned the last attempt. This is the new timeline."

The Priest bowed his head. "Very well. I will inform the others."

"Be patient. I have everything under control." Just let me do my part. This is hard enough for me as it is without the continued meddling.

"Let me know when you have an update."

Banks nodded. "I will."

‹ CHAPTER 13 ›

Kate was snuggled up against Cris in the crook of his arm, a position he'd come to know well and cherish over their two months together. They fit perfectly, in a way he'd never imagined possible. *What will I do without her?* The departure for their internships was only a little over a week away; a countdown he'd rather forget.

Kate reoriented in Cris' arms, bringing her face close to his. "You know," she began, kissing him between words, "we have the place to ourselves tonight."

Cris kissed her back, his mind racing. *Stars! Is she suggesting…? Since we're about to leave, I didn't think I'd have to worry about that now!* Thus far, he had been careful to hold back and not take things too far, knowing they'd soon need to part ways for their internships. But, bit by bit, the physicality of their relationship was progressing despite his efforts. His resistance was twofold. First, there was the Tararian custom for highborn to maintain chastity until engagement—a custom that didn't seem to be a high priority for Kate as a fourth child. While he wasn't overly concerned with tradition, the truth about his identity was another matter. *How can I even consider being with her in that way when she doesn't even know who I really am?*

"You can stay the night, if you want." She moved her hands over his chest, working their way downward.

No, not yet! "Kate, I'd really love to stay, but I have a report I should work on."

"That can wait." She continued to run her hands over his body, knowing just where to touch. "Before we go away, I want you to be my first." Her eyes searched his, looking for affirmation. "I lo—"

No mistaking that! Cris throbbed with desire, but he resisted—barely. *I can't...* "I really have to go. I'll see you soon." He extracted himself from her and gave her a quick kiss before rushing out the door.

"Cris, wait!"

Keep it together. As soon as he was in the hallway, he located an alcove and ducked out of sight. He leaned against the wall, fighting the competing impulses within. *Why now? I know I need to tell her who I am first, but this isn't the right time. I just wanted to go on the internship and deal with all this when we get back.* He steadied himself and made his way quickly to his quarters. *Shite, I should have anticipated this.*

Cris closed the door and sunk to the floor, his back against the wall in the common room.

Stars! Maybe I do need to tell her before we go. But how? I'm in so deep now, this could ruin everything. His pulse raced.

Scott walked out of his bedroom. "Hey. Wait, what's wrong?"

Cris tried to talk but couldn't force anything out. He hid his face in his hands.

Scott walked over. "Cris, what is it?"

Cris shook his head. "I haven't been honest with you. With anyone."

"What do you mean?"

Cris rose slowly, still leaning against the wall for support. "Truths have a way of getting lost sometimes. Buried. And once you start down that path, it's hard to turn away."

"I don't like it when you start getting all philosophical on me. What's going on?" Scott looked concerned. He leaned against the couch across from Cris.

"It's Kate. Things have gotten serious between us. She's wanting to take it that next level."

"That's great!"

Cris shook his head. "It would be, but…" He searched for the words. "She thinks I'm someone I'm not. I don't know if she'll accept me for who I really am, and that terrifies me. I can't lose her." *I love her. Stars, I love her so much. More than I ever thought I could. Why didn't I just tell her the truth from the beginning?*

Scott looked confused. "Why, what did you tell her?"

Cris shook his head. "It's what I *didn't* tell her. I never lied. Not to her, or you, or anyone. You need to know that."

"Okay. So what's the issue?"

Cris swallowed. *Do I tell him? Gah, I have to tell someone or I'm going to explode.* "Scott, I don't want this to change anything. You're one of the first real friends I've ever had. That means so much to me."

"You too, man. Nothing could come between us."

Cris nodded. "Well, you know how I said I was from Sieten? That's true. But what I didn't mention was where I lived outside the city… At the Sietinen estate."

Scott's face drained. "What are you saying?"

"I'm the heir to the Third Region. I'm Cristoph Sietinen."

Scott worked his mouth. Shaking his head.

"Scott…"

Scott held up his hand. "I just need a minute." He paced on the far side of the room. "Heir to Sietinen, really?"

Cris nodded. "I swear it."

"Well shite." Scott paused. "Wait, so I unwittingly played matchmaker for the High Dynasties?"

Cris nearly collapsed into nervous laughter. He regained some semblance of composure. "It would seem so."

"Bomax."

Both men were distant, chewing unconsciously on their lower lips. They didn't know whether to laugh or run away from each other. Cris felt relief at releasing one of his most guarded secrets, but he felt for his friend. Scott just looked lost.

Eventually, Scott tousled his hair and sat down on the couch. He was coming to terms. "You have to tell Kate."

Cris sat down on the couch across from him. "I know."

"She's crazy about you. You know that, right?"

Cris nodded. *I can only hope it's enough to see past my deception. I need to think of what to say...* "I'll tell her tomorrow."

‹ CHAPTER 14 ›

The pit in Cris' stomach was even deeper than the night before. His only solace was that Scott had been surprisingly casual about everything that morning, so perhaps there was hope.

After completing his work for the day, Cris went to Kate's quarters, knowing what he had to say but hating that reality. He hit the buzzer, ready to accept the fate he was dealt.

Kate practically leaped into Cris' arms the moment the door was open. "You left so suddenly last night!" She kissed him with untamed passion. "Must have been a busy day. I didn't see you at breakfast or lunch. "

Cris held her close. *I needed to wait until we could talk alone.* "I'm sorry. I hate being apart from you." *And soon we'll have to say goodbye for who knows how long.*

Kate led him inside with her arm still around him. She directed him onto the couch and climbed onto his lap, straddling him. "I really don't want to be apart from you anymore. In any way." She slid her hands down his stomach, stopping tantalizingly close to his groin, her eyes filled with desire.

Don't give in. It took everything to keep Cris from giving in to her advances, but he held back. "Kate, there's something we need to talk about."

Kate leaned forward and whispered in his ear. "Talking can wait."

Cris took her hands and slid her onto the couch next to him. "Not this." Kate tried to protest, but he was persistent. "We've been spending a lot of time together recently. I feel like we've really gotten to know each other, and you're such a beautiful person, inside and out. You mean so much to me."

Kate smiled. "You mean a lot to me, too. I think you're amazing."

Cris forced a smile through his nerves. "But the thing is, you're from a High Dynasty."

Kate shook her head. "That doesn't matter, I told you. None of that matters here."

"Isn't there a part of you that holds onto that old life?"

"No, this is my life now."

Cris took a deep breath. "What I'm trying to say is, would you really spend your life with me, even marry me, knowing I'd be nothing more than a TSS Agent?"

Kate searched his eyes. "Are you proposing?"

Cris blushed and let go of her hands. *That wasn't the reaction I was expecting!* "No. I mean, not formally. More hypothetically."

Kate was silent, but her elation was apparent by the upturn at the corners of her mouth and fire in her eyes. "If you're asking if I think such an arrangement would be 'beneath me', no. I never had aspirations of marrying within the Dynasties. There was a single eligible suitor for someone of my birthright, but he would never so much as meet me."

"He was an idiot." *I was that idiot.*

"Regardless, none of that ever mattered to me. All I want is to be happy. To have someone who's as crazy about me as I am about him. I can say with absolute certainty that you make me happier than anyone ever has. You're all I think about."

Cris smiled, reveling in the connection between them that he couldn't put into words. "You too."

Kate gave him a coy grin. "So yes, in this hypothetical of

yours, I would happily marry you."

Cris leaned forward and kissed her. He couldn't help himself. *You still need to tell her.* He pulled himself away. "That means more to me than you know."

"Why are you so nervous?" She took his hands in hers.

"I wasn't completely upfront with you about who I am. I've phrased things in a way to give you a certain impression about me. I feel awful about it, Kate. I shouldn't have, but I just needed to know you care about *me*, not who I am by reputation." He looked into her eyes, trying to make everything okay.

"All right…"

"Kate, my real name is Cristoph Sietinen. And I'm very much in love with you."

"You're…?" She pulled back.

Without hesitation, Cris pushed up the sleeve on his left forearm and turned the inside of his wrist upward for her to examine his Mark to confirm his identity. Instinctually, she pulled out her handheld and tuned the light to the closely guarded frequency that everyone born into a High Dynasty had memorized practically since birth. Kate ran the light over his wrist, and the Sietinen crest and Cris' full birth name glowed light purple on the surface of his skin.

"It's true…" Kate ran her fingers over the Mark, tracing the form of the serpent in his family's emblem; she touched the falcon invisibly imprinted on her own wrist. She caught herself. "You lied to me."

"Kate—"

"No, you lied to me. Call it 'withholding the truth' or whatever you want to tell yourself, but that's a bomaxed big of a thing to keep from someone!"

Uh oh. "I know it was stupid of me. When I found out who you were, I panicked. I've been 'Cris Sights' for so long now, it's my default."

Kate scoffed. "It's one thing to introduce yourself that way, but to wait until you propose? Stars! I almost gave myself to you." She stood up and stepped away.

Cris rose, but gave her space. "I just needed to be sure."

"About what?"

"That you were interested in me as a person, not my title."

Kate stared at him with disbelief. "You think I'm really that shallow? After everything we've discussed?"

"No. I..." *Shite! How do I salvage this?* He took a breath. "I didn't have very good experiences with other Dynasties in the past."

"After our first date you should have had more faith in me." She crossed her arms. "And especially after a few weeks."

"I did. There never seemed like the right time to tell you."

Kate looked like she wanted to cry. "Oh really? Not when I was pouring my heart out to you about my own crappy childhood on Tararia? Or talking about my poor sister whose betrothed—your *brother*—died? Or when we speculated about a new Taran revolution?"

"Well... yes." *Fok, this is bad.*

Kate laughed to herself, fury building in her eyes. "Let's not overlook the fact that my suitor on Tararia was *you*. You cast me aside without ever giving me a chance."

"I maintain that I was an idiot."

"It seems you still are."

Cris winced. "I meant everything I said. I do love you, and I want to spend my life with you."

"I thought I did, too." Kate pulled into herself, the anger written on her face turning to hurt. "One of the things I liked so much about you was that you were a regular guy, yet you were cultured and self-assured, even around someone like me. You had big ideas. But I now realize it was just the same self-serving arrogance of anyone else in the High Dynasties."

"I ran away because I didn't want to be like them!"

Kate shook her head. "That's what makes it even worse. At

least most people think on behalf of their family, but you acted completely in your own self-interest. You abandoned people who were counting on you. It's selfish and cowardly."

No! They forced me out. They didn't want me... "It wasn't like that."

"Deny it all you want, but you're acting just like the people you profess to despise—thinking that you can say or do whatever you want, and then announce yourself as a dynastic heir and expect everything to magically work out."

No... "I just got so wrapped up in escaping that life—"

"You haven't escaped! If anything, you've become even more like them."

By pledging my life to the TSS? By wanting to bring down the Priesthood? Right! "How can you say that?"

"Charming and cultured on the surface, but you're only in it for yourself. I thought you could be a real partner—someone who saw the other side and believed things could be different."

"I do feel that way! Together we could—"

"Yeah, we could have done a lot. Some of the things you said really got me thinking. But now I don't know if I can trust you. You didn't even tell me your real name—how much else have you kept from me?"

"Nothing!"

"I don't know..."

"Kate, please try to understand my reasons and where I was coming from."

"I think you should go."

Cris' heart dropped. "Can't we talk this through?"

Kate shook her head, staring past the floor. "There's nothing to talk about. I need some time to think."

I can't leave things like this, not so close to leaving for our internships. "Kate, please." Cris took a step forward and held out his arms for a hug, but Kate held up her hand in protest.

"Don't touch me. Just go."

Reluctantly, Cris nodded. *I don't want to make things worse.* "I'm sorry." He let himself out.

Cris' stomach was in writhing knots. *How do I fix this?* He hurried back to his quarters, avoiding the gaze of other Junior Agents in the hall. If he couldn't be with Kate, then he wanted to be alone. To his disappointment, he found Scott sprawled on his favorite couch in the common room of their quarters.

"Hey," Scott greeted when he entered. "I thought you'd be at Kate's for the night."

The knots in Cris' stomach pulled tighter. "Things didn't go well."

Scott sat up. "You told her?"

"And now she hates me."

"Oh shite."

Cris eased himself onto the adjacent couch. "Yeah."

"What happened?"

It all feels like a nightmare now. "I told her I loved her and wanted to spend my life with her—"

"Whoa, you didn't tell me that part before!"

Cris ignored the interjection. "When it was clear she felt the same way, I told her who I was. She's furious I misled her."

Scott let out of a slow breath. "That was a lot of revelations all at once."

"I really foked up." Cris rubbed his eyes with the heels of his hands.

Scott shrugged. "I suppose that depends on how you look at it. Maybe she never even would have talked to you, if she'd known who you were upfront."

"You're not helping." Cris glared at his friend.

"My point is," Scott continued, "you might have missed out on seeing what you could have together. But now you both know. The connection is obvious, even to an outside observer like me. Don't give up."

"I'm not. I just wish things were different." *Stars! Why did I ever let it go this long without telling her the truth? That was so stupid.*

"Give her some time." Scott gave him a supportive smile.

"Yeah." *I can't talk about this anymore or I'm going to drive myself crazy.* Cris rose. "I'll see you tomorrow."

"Hang in there."

Cris felt like banging his head against his bedroom wall, but tried to bury the feeling. At first, he laid down on his bed, but it was soon apparent that he was far too wound up to sleep. With a frustrated groan, he forced himself up to grab his tablet off of the desk.

There was a notification that he had several unread messages in his inbox. His first instinct was to ignore them and try to distract himself with a mindless game. *But what if Kate wrote me?* Gritting his teeth, he opened the inbox.

Most of the messages were an email chain amongst some of his classmates regarding a group assignment. He scanned through the inbox. *Nothing from Kate.* He sighed. Then, he noticed one message in the list unlike the others. It was addressed from his father, with the subject: "I want to talk to you."

As if this day could get any worse. It had been a while since he'd received anything from his parents. With a groan, he decided to open the message. The body read: "You can't ignore me forever. Next time I call, please answer." *He's the last person I want to talk to right now.* Cris was about to close the message when he noticed that it was tagged with an automatic "read" receipt back to the sender. *Great, now he'll know I'm at my computer.*

Sure enough, an incoming call from Tararia popped up on the viewscreen above his desktop. Cris wanted to decline, but he knew if his father was serious about reaching him, he would keep trying until he got through. *If I just hear him out, then maybe he'll leave me alone.*

Cris settled into his desk chair and initiated the video call. "Hello, Father."

The image of Reinen appeared on the screen. His hair was a little more touched with gray than Cris remembered. "Hi, Cris. I didn't actually expect you to answer."

Any other day and I probably wouldn't have. "You seemed pretty insistent."

"Well, I'm glad you did." Reinen looked him over. "I try to forget how long it's been, but seeing you now... You've grown up."

Cris crossed his arms. "Well, it has been almost five years."

"Did you get him?" came Cris' mother's voice from out of the camera's view. Alana came to stand next to her husband. "Cris! We've been so worried about you." She was a regal woman, touched by the years, but carrying them with grace.

A full-on family reunion. "Hello, Mother." *I'm surprised she has any interest in seeing me.*

"You look well." Reinen ventured a smile.

"I'm well enough." *Everything was great until yesterday.* He suppressed the ache in his chest as his thoughts started to drift back to Kate.

"Is everything okay?" Alana asked.

Reinen searched his son's face. "Are you happy?"

They see your pain. Don't let them bait you. "Happier than I ever was there."

Alana paused. "We miss you, Cris."

I find that hard to believe. "Look, I've had a pretty shitey day. What do you want?" Cris snapped.

Alana looked aghast and turned away.

Reinen recoiled. "We just wanted to wish you a happy birthday."

Birthday? Cris glanced at the calendar on his computer. *Stars! It is. With everything going on, I completely forgot my own birthday.* He looked down. *I just assumed they had an ulterior motive.*

"You're our only child to make it to twenty-one," Reinen added faintly.

Now I feel like a jerk. "I... Thanks."

"We'd have a party for you, but..." Alana said, still looking down.

I'm not there. "I know." Cris took a deep breath. *I abandoned them and didn't look back.* Despite his own feelings of discontent, he knew it wasn't a fair thing to have done to his parents. Kate's words were still fresh in his mind. "I'm sorry I left with no explanation. I was only thinking of myself."

Reinen was caught off-guard. "It's nice to hear you acknowledge that," he said eventually.

"It wasn't until recently that I had the proper perspective." *Kate was right about me, as much as I didn't want to admit it.*

Reinen sighed. "All these years I've tried to understand."

"It wasn't any one reason." Cris ran a hand through his hair. *I can't possibly explain to him what it felt like to be an outcast in my own family.*

"Alana, dear, will you give us a moment?" Reinen gently placed his hands on his wife's shoulders and directed her away.

"It was good to see you, Cris. Please stay in touch," Alana said as she turned to go.

Cris doubted it was a genuine request. "Goodbye, Mother."

Reinen gathered himself as soon as Alana had departed. "I still wish you would come home."

"Please, don't start—" *Can't we just talk without it turning into a lecture?*

"What kind of life can you possibly have there?" Reinen's eyes narrowed.

Cris had to fight to keep from immediately going on the defensive. *He does have a right to be angry with me. I ran away from my responsibilities.* "The TSS has given me something I couldn't get anywhere else. I finally have friends here with the same abilities. I feel like I belong here."

Reinen began to pace across the room and the camera followed his movement. "That was fine for a while, but at some point you need to assume your proper place in society. You're a dynastic heir! You need to start acting like one."

Cris glared at the image of his father. *The sentimental act was all a facade after all.* "There's more to me than my social standing."

"Regardless, you need to look at your marriage prospects. I can't imagine you have a great selection within the TSS."

Cris smirked. "You'd be surprised."

Reinen stared down his son. "I won't let this bloodline be destroyed by you trying to marry a commoner."

He hasn't changed at all! "Thank you for reminding me why I left Tararia in the first place."

"You're meant for more than this, Cris," Reinen implored.

I am. Just not in the way you think. "Don't bother calling me again." Cris ended the transmission with a disgusted groan. *No wonder I was so self-centered. That man was my role model.*

He returned to his bed and stared up at the ceiling. *I won't be that kind of person. At least the TSS has pointed me in the right direction. I wish Kate could see that.* He rolled over on his side. *The TSS is still my new home, with or without Kate. But I hope it's "with"...*

◄   CHAPTER 15   ►

Still nothing from Kate. *Is she going to avoid me forever?* After three days of obsessively checking his email and receiving no message, Cris was beginning to despair.

The conversation with his father had left Cris feeling bitter, and it made him miss Kate's companionship even more. He had tried to keep himself busy with class work, but he was cracking. After finishing up his remaining assignments for the day, Cris headed into the common room of his quarters to find Scott.

To his relief, Scott appeared to be done with his own assignments and was playing a game on his tablet while sprawled across the couch.

"Hey," Cris greeted.

"You want something," Scott replied.

He's perceptive. "Has Marsie said anything about Kate? I'm losing my mind."

Scott set down his tablet. "I told you, you need to be patient."

Cris groaned. "But has she said anything?"

"Just that Kate was really upset. I haven't talked to her since the day after your little blowout."

That's not helpful. Cris collapsed on the couch and crossed his arms. "I don't know what to do."

Scott let out an exaggerated sighed. "You're going to drive *me* crazy if you keep this up! Try to track her down in one of the lounges or mess hall if you're so intent on talking to her."

Yes! A seemingly random encounter. "That's a great idea."

Scott shook his head with exasperation. "Try not to get into deeper trouble."

Cris grabbed his tablet out of his room. *I can look like I'm just going to study in the lounge.* It was a feeble plan, but he was desperate.

Intent on the mission at hand, Cris set out to comb the common Junior Agent recreation areas.

The first three locations were a bust. Cris was on his way to the mess hall when he spotted Kate at the end of the corridor.

His heart leaped. "Kate!"

She turned away to walk the other direction, but Cris jogged over to her before she could find an exit. "I still need more time," Kate said as Cris approached. She kept her gaze down.

I can't wait any longer. We leave in three days. "I miss you."

Kate sighed and looked up at Cris. "I miss you, too." She groaned, seemingly frustrated with herself.

Cris wouldn't let her look away. "Can we talk? Please?"

After a moment, Kate yielded. "Fine."

Progress! "Come on." Cris headed down the hall toward a row of study rooms. He led Kate into an empty one.

"You really hurt me, you know," Kate said as soon as the door was closed.

Cris set his tablet down on the table. "I'm sorry. I didn't mean to."

Kate took a deep breath. "I know you didn't." She crossed her arms. "This isn't easy for me."

"It wasn't right of me to keep my identity from you."

Kate shook her head. "It's not just that. I'd already mentally left behind my life on Tararia and committed to the TSS. I didn't think I'd ever look back."

"I have no intention of leaving the TSS, either."

"But, like it or not, you're still an heir. You'll have two

lives—one here, and one out there. If I'm with you, that means I will still have a responsibility to Tararia, too. I couldn't have the clean break that I'd envisioned. Especially not if you were serious about that plan of yours."

I hadn't thought about that part of it. "I was serious—we could have two votes between our families, when the time comes. But, you're right. It was a lot of me to ask of you."

"No wonder you had thought it through. I should have known then that you were high-born." She sighed. "I guess these last few days have surfaced a lot of bad memories from Tararia, from back when I felt like I didn't have any direction."

"I'm so sorry, Kate." Cris brushed her cheek with his finger.

She shrugged him off. "You should have been upfront with me."

"I know. You were absolutely right about what you said. I was thinking only of myself." He took her hands; she didn't resist. "When I ran away from Tararia, I didn't know that also meant running away from you. At the time, I felt like I had to get away, at any cost. My parents... Tristen's accident devastated them. I knew they had me out of necessity, not want. All my life, they looked right through me, or when they did see me, I saw them wishing I was someone else."

Kate nodded. "I would have run away, too, if they hadn't let me go. I'm surprised yours let you stay here."

"Hah! My father writes me at least once a month begging me to come home."

"Oh."

"Everything about Tararia was toxic. I know I've brought up some pretty revolutionary ideas at times, but I honestly believe there's an opportunity for real change. Being here at the TSS is a chance to buy time and leverage." Cris caught her gaze. "I promise you, I may have left out my birth name and title, but the rest has been all me."

Kate searched his face. "So you really meant it, about

wanting to be with me?"

"Absolutely, I want nothing more than to have you as a life partner."

Kate squeezed his hands. "I forgive you."

Without hesitation, Cris pulled her in for a kiss. She relaxed into him, releasing the anxious tension of the last few days. After a few moments, Cris pulled away just enough to look Kate in the eye. "I promise to never mislead you again. I love you."

"I love you, too. We can do so much together."

Cris' heart skipped a beat with the words. *To think I could have lost her... I'll never make that mistake again.*

Kate grinned. "But you should work on your proposal technique, because your first one kind of sucked."

"Don't worry, the real one will be much better."

<>

A great weight had been lifted. Kate had accepted him, even if things hadn't gone quite like Cris imagined. *Then again, I didn't think anything through.*

Still, Cris knew better than to believe all challenges were behind him. His relationship with Kate would be difficult within the TSS. It was one thing to casually date, but marriages among Agents were extremely rare. Furthermore, they would no doubt face long periods of separation—first with their impending internships, and after graduation, any random assignment could keep them away from each other for unthinkable spans. Then there was the matter of their parents. *One step at a time.*

The most immediate need was having the High Commander officially sanction the relationship; without that, many other factors would be moot. Cris grabbed his tablet off his desk and sat down on the bed to draft an email to Banks, requesting a meeting. Given the unusual subject matter, he kept the message brief and somewhat vague. In the back of his mind, Cris knew he would leave the TSS before giving up Kate, but hopefully it wouldn't come to such an ultimatum. Nonetheless, he felt a twinge of dread as he sent the message.

Cris set the tablet down next to him on the bed and sprawled out. He yawned and settled into the pillows. A nap was very appealing, having stayed up well past curfew to talk with Kate after reconciling. It was a necessary conversation, and it had left him feeling even closer to her.

As soon as Cris closed his eyes, he heard an email notification chirp. *Response from Banks already?* His heart skipped. Propped up on his elbows, Cris read the new message. It was indeed from the High Commander, and it stated that he was free to meet at the start of the hour. *That's in 10 minutes!* Cris jumped up from the bed. *So much for preparing a thoughtful speech.*

Cris rushed out of his quarters and took the elevator up to Level 1. He arrived at the High Commander's office a couple minutes early and found the door open.

Banks was examining his desktop inside, and he looked up when Cris approached the door. He gestured Cris in. "You may close the door, if you like."

Cris entered and took Banks' offer. "Thank you for agreeing to meet with me on such short notice, sir."

Banks smiled. "You caught me on a good day. Have a seat."

"Thank you, sir." Cris sat down across from Banks in one of the two guest chairs facing the desk—cozy leather seats with padded arms that gave a homey feel to the room.

"What can I do for you?" Banks asked, examining Cris through his steepled fingers.

Cris swallowed. "This is admittedly kind of awkward. I'm not sure what to ask, exactly."

Banks cocked his head. "You had some reason for meeting with me."

"Well…" *Just say it.* "I'm not sure if you're aware or not, but Kate Vaenetri and I have been seeing each other for a few months now. And, we've decided we'd like to get married."

Banks' eyes widened behind his tinted glasses and he sat up straighter in his chair as he folded his hands on the desktop. "That's some big news."

"It's all happened rather quickly." *I had no idea my entire life would change like this, but already it's hard to believe it was ever any other way.*

"Congratulations are in order," Banks said with a smile.

"Thank you, sir, but it's not quite official yet. I still need to get her a ring, and somehow convince our parents to go along with it." *That's going to be a fun conversation.*

The High Commander looked intrigued. "A starstone ring, I imagine."

Cris nodded. *That's one tradition I won't break.* A privilege only for the High Dynasties, such stones were rare to the point of being incomprehensibly expensive. "Yes, I'll need to go in person."

"I guess I'll finally get to see one up close. I hear they're breathtaking."

"They are. She's definitely earned it, putting up with me."

Banks smiled. "Well, I'll grant you the leave whenever you need it. I know wedding planning is stressful enough without having to worry about getting time away from work."

That's a relief. "Thank you, sir. That's still a ways off, but I wanted to talk to you as soon as possible, since I know this sort of thing is unusual within the TSS."

Banks steepled his fingers again. "It is, yes. Then again, we don't get many High Dynasty trainees."

Cris shifted in his chair and looked down. "I don't mean to place you in a tough spot."

"No, not at all," Banks assured. "The lack of long-term relationships among Agents is self-imposed more than any TSS policy."

It can't be easy. Are we crazy to try? "I'm glad it's not a direct violation of anything."

Banks shook his head. "Far from it. Many Agents do settle down, eventually—often with a local after an extended planetary assignment. Those people don't pass through Headquarters very often, though. You'll definitely be an anomaly around here."

I'm used to feeling out of place. "Is there any way to guarantee an assignment together?"

"Of course, Cris. I wouldn't send you off to opposite sides of the galaxy."

"Thank you, sir."

Banks leaned forward against the desk. "In all honesty, you will likely stay right here."

Cris came to attention. "Oh?"

"You're on pace to have the highest Course Test score on record." Banks gave him the hint of an approving smile. "That'll put you far up in the Command ranks."

Cris sat in shock for a moment. "Sir, I'm not sure what to say."

"You can be very proud of yourself."

"Thank you, sir." *I wasn't expecting a leadership role immediately after graduation.*

Banks paused. "I'll do what I can to make sure you and Kate can have a happy family life here."

Family? "I wasn't really thinking that far ahead."

"I have to. I know you're a dynastic heir, and that comes with a responsibility to your bloodline."

"I suppose it does." *Stars! That always seemed so far away, and now it's just around the corner.*

"Besides, it's probably for the best that you be here, at Headquarters, when that time comes."

"Why's that, sir?" *Not that I'd want to raise a kid on Tararia after my experience, but this isn't exactly an ideal setting, either.*

"I can only imagine a child of yours will be… extraordinary," Banks stated, seeming to choose his words carefully.

"What do you mean?"

Banks hesitated. "Your father was the first in recent generations to have abilities, correct?"

Abilities he pretended not to have. "Yes, I believe so."

"That makes you 9th Generation. As far as I know, Kate is, as well. So, your child would be 10th Generation on both sides, which is typically the peak of ability. And since you're two of the most gifted I've ever seen, I can only imagine what the combination would produce."

Cris swallowed. "I hadn't thought about it."

"I didn't mean to worry you with idle speculation."

"No, sir. Just caught me off guard a little." *Stars! What kind of parent will I be?*

Banks waved off the comment. "Well anyway, consider your request approved. Sorry to have jumped ahead."

"Thank you, sir." *I'll try to be a better father than mine was to me. No matter what, I can offer love and support. Unconditionally.*

"As for the wedding," Banks continued, "would it be possible for you to wait until after graduation? With the internship departures in just a couple days..."

I'd marry her right now before we go if I could, but we need to be practical. "I agree. It would be best to wait."

Banks nodded. "Okay, good. We can work out any administrative details later on. Thank you for coming to me with this."

"Of course, sir."

Banks caught his gaze. "Please, let me know if you ever need anything."

Something tells me he isn't that friendly with all the trainees. "Thank you, I will."

"Take care, Cris."

Cris nodded his thanks and showed himself out. *I guess that went well?* He had no doubt that the coming years would be difficult at times, but at least he could take comfort in knowing he'd have a partner to share it with—and, apparently, an advocate.

He smiled to himself. *I can have a life here. A family. This is what I always wanted, even when I didn't know it yet.*

<>   <>   <>

Banks could hardly contain himself until Cris left the room. *I can't believe it's all coming together. After all these years.*

Banks called his contact at the Priesthood on the viewscreen.

The Priest answered after several seconds. "Yes?"

"I have excellent news," Banks said with a smile. "Cristoph Sietinen just approached me with plans to wed Katrine Vaenetri."

The Priest's grin was visible beneath the hood of his robe. "We were beginning to worry they would never meet."

"It was inevitable their connection would bring them together eventually," Banks replied.

"True."

"And Cris agreed to wait until after graduation for the wedding. That will allow us to ensure their position as contracted Agents. It will give us leverage against the Dynasties to keep them here at Headquarters."

"Very foresightful."

"I do have one concern," Banks continued. "We've had to move Kate through the training program quickly, to keep her in the same cohort as Cris. I've arranged for her to keep training while on her internship—hopefully it's enough to catch her up. But, she still might not score an accurate CR on the Course Test."

"Accurate scoring is not a high priority in this matter."

"My concern is that she'll score below her potential and not justify her Primus Command rank." *The only way to ensure them assignments together without drawing suspicion.*

"Then make sure she does. It's imperative they are secure in their relationship and feel comfortable enough to bear the Cadicle—your Primus Elite—as soon as possible."

The result of our generations of planning and manipulation. "What do we do until then?" *It'll still be decades before a child will be grown and ready to come into the war.* "Our forces can't hold out against the Bakzen in the rift for much longer. We need more Agent recruits if we're to last until then."

The Priest thought for a moment. "Perhaps now it is time to once again embrace such abilities—change the public consciousness to revere the TSS and the duty it serves. Maybe the denouncement of telekinetic powers has outlived its usefulness."

People have finally forgotten that those abilities were once core to our race, and how they came to be lost. "Thank you, that has been my hope for many years. Such a change would be to our benefit in winning the war."

"Consider it done." The Priest looked Banks in the eye. "But the true nature of the war must remain our best kept secret."

Banks looked at the floor, uncomfortable under the Priest's intense gaze. *So few others know the truth I must guard, but it is a necessary burden.* "I faithfully serve Tararia and the Priesthood."

ACKNOWLEDGEMENTS

Thank you to all of my family and friends who made this book possible. Foremost, without the encouragement of my lift partner, Nick, most of this story would still only exist in my head. His support, advocacy and companionship are my greatest inspiration. I owe my surrogate sister, Jess, for giving me the nudge to continue after she reviewed the very first draft of what would eventually evolve into this series. Thank you to my friend, Anthony, for bringing the visual elements of the story to life, and for always lending a critical eye. Special thanks to Steve for believing in me, and also to Collin, Annie, Amy, Jenna, John, and Bethany for helping me add the final polish. Finally, thank you to my parents, Randy and Deborah, for giving me everything I needed to let me follow my dreams.

GLOSSARY

Agent - A class of officer within the TSS reserved for those with telekinetic and telepathic gifts. There are three levels of Agent based on level of ability: Primus, Sacon and Trion.

Bakzen - A militaristic race living beyond the outer colonies. Little is known about the Bakzen, other than they are alien in customs and appearance compared to Tarans.

Cadicle - The definition of individual perfection in the Priesthood's founding ideology, with emergence of the Cadicle heralding the start to the next stage of evolution for the Taran race.

Course Rank (CR) - The official measurement of an Agent's ability level, taken at the end of their training immediately before graduation from Junior Agent to Agent. The Course Rank Test is a multi-phase examination, including direct focusing of telekinetic energy into a testing sphere. The magnitude of energy focused during the exercise is the primary factor dictating the Agent's CR.

Earth - A planet occupied by Humans, a divergent race of Tarans. Considered a "lost colony," Earth is not recognized as part of the Taran government.

High Commander - The officer responsible for the administration of the TSS. Always an Agent from the Primus class.

High Dynasties - Six families on Tararia that control the corporations critical to the functioning of Taran society. The "Big Six" each have a designated Region on Tararia, which is the seat of their power. The Dynasties in aggregate form an oligarchical government for the Taran colonies.

Initiate - The second stage of the TSS training program for Agents. A trainee will typically remain at the Initiate stage for two or three years.

Jump Drive - The engine system for travel through subspace. Conventional jump drives require an interface with the SiNavTech navigation system and subspace navigation beacons.

Junior Agent - The third stage of the TSS training program for Agents. A trainee will typically remain at the Junior Agent stage for three to five years.

Lead Agent - The highest ranking Agent and second in command to the High Commander. The Lead Agent is responsible for overseeing the Agent training program and frequently serves as a liaison for TSS business with Taran colonies.

Lower Dynasties - There are 247 recognized Lower Dynasties in Taran society. Many of these families have a presence on Tararia, but some are residents of the other inner colonies.

Sacon - The middle tier of TSS Agents. Typically, Sacon Agents will score a CR between 6 and 7.9.

Tarans - The general term for all individuals with genetic relation to Tararian ancestry. Several divergent races are recognized by their planet or system.

Tararia - The home planet for the Taran race and seat of the central government.

Tararian Selective Service (TSS) - A military organization with two divisions: (1) Agent Class, and (2) Militia Class.

Agents possess telekinetic and telepathic abilities; the TSS is the only place where individuals with such gifts can gain official training. The Militia class offers a formal training program for those without telekinetic abilities, providing tactical and administrative support to Agents. The Headquarters is located inside the moon of the planet Earth. Additional Militia training facilities are located throughout the Taran colonies.

Trainee - The generic term for a student of the TSS, and also the term for first year Agent students (when capitalized Trainee). Students are not fully "initiated" into the TSS until their second year.

Trion - The lowest tier of TSS Agents. Typically, Trion Agents will score a CR below 5.9.

Priesthood of the Cadicle - A formerly theological institution responsible for oversight of all governmental affairs and the flow of information throughout the Taran colonies. The Priesthood has jurisdiction over even the High Dynasties and provides a tiebreaking vote on new initiatives proposed by the High Dynasty oligarchy.

Primus - The highest of three Agent classes within the TSS, reserved for those with the strongest telekinetic abilities. Typically, Primus Agents will score a CR above 8.

ABOUT THE AUTHOR

Amy has always loved science fiction—books, movies, shows and games. After devouring some of the classics like *Dune* and *Ender's Game* in her tween years, she began writing short stories.

In the ensuing years, Amy attended the Vancouver School of Arts and Academics in Vancouver, Washington, where she studied creative writing. She eventually became a Psychology major at Portland State University, but also pursued a minor in Professional Writing. After graduating, she stumbled into a career as a proposal manager.

Amy currently lives in Portland, Oregon. When she's not writing, she enjoys travel, wine tasting, binge-watching TV series and playing epic strategy board games.

Made in the USA
San Bernardino, CA
31 October 2017